How to Raise a Juvenile Delinquent:

A Common Sense Approach to Parenting

Amber White

A&D Press

ISBN: 1-59526-647-X

Printed in the United States of America by A&D Press

Library of Congress Control Number: 2006908396

How to Raise a Juvenile Delinquent:

A Common Sense Approach to Parenting

Dedication

For my husband, Dean, who paid for
this book in more ways than one.
I love you immeasurably.

Disclaimer

The purpose of this book is to entertain and educate. Experience and opinion formulate much of the information presented. Some of the content may not present popular opinions or be politically correct. The reader may or may not agree with the book's content.

It is not the author's intent to render professional help, but to provide a point of view procured through life and job experience. Every effort has been made to ensure that the content of this book is accurate; however, there may be errors. The material should be used with other sources of information. The author and publisher shall have neither responsibility nor liability to any entity or person for damage or loss alleged to have been caused directly or indirectly because of reading this book.

About the Author

Amber White is a mother of two young boys. She has worked at juvenile hall since 1997 as a deputy probation counselor and deputy probation officer. Prior to working with youth in juvenile hall, she worked at various group homes and dealt with severely emotionally disturbed adolescents.

After graduating from California State Dominguez Hills with a degree in psychology, Amber knew she wanted to work in probation with children. She has dedicated the last nine years to bringing about positive changes in the community's youth by practicing respect, accountability, and deterrence to those she assists. Amber has consistently provided education, life skills, structure, and counseling with caring objectivity to hundreds of youthful offenders.

During the course of Amber's career, she has observed many dysfunctional families and situations. After countless interviews of incarcerated youth and their parents, Amber concluded that the parents all exhibit the same patterns of behavior that ultimately contribute to their child's delinquency. From this, Amber was able to identify ten of the most common problematic parenting styles and offer solutions.

Amber wrote this book in an attempt to relieve pressures and frustrations with the lack of respect, accountability, and deterrence members of our society offer one another. She attempts to stay optimistic by exploring problems and offering solutions, rather than excuses.

Acknowledgements

I would most like to thank those who believed in me, especially my loving husband, who thought my ideas were valuable, valid, and obtainable. I would like to thank my loving family, who helped create the person I am today. Thanks for all of the spankings, Mom! I am a better person for them. My colleagues Pauline Scarano, Timothy Cole, Elaine Robison, Amoreena Brady, Jerry O'Leary, Terri Poche, Moraima Walkingstick, Lynn Haller, Luis Hernandez, and Jim Riley all offered support and encouragement. I would like to also acknowledge my colleague and friend, Bryan Wagstaff, who was a constant sounding board for this book and offered constructive criticism and encouragement throughout its writing.

Also, special thanks to Jill at JillPetersonphotography.com who easily captured my vision for the cover and aptly titled the book. To my friend turned mentor, Lisa McLaughlin, special thanks for your editing expertise, which truly transformed this project. Your patience, skill, and ability to point out all the "mean-sounding" verbiage were priceless.

I would also like to thank the scores of children with whom I have worked. Thank you for giving me purpose. Thank you for making me laugh and continue to care. Thank you for forging on, despite the hand you were dealt. Remember not to make excuses for yourself or your behavior. Believe in yourself, and you can accomplish anything!

Working in probation and dealing with at-risk youth has been one of the most fulfilling, gratifying accomplishments of my life. I truly believe in the role probation plays in the community and believe that anyone who wants to change can be rehabilitated.

Contents

Prologue

This book began as a series of random rants. For the past two years, I slowly accumulated my feelings and opinions on paper. It was the only way to vent feelings of frustration with the system and society. Soon, I had mounds of "chicken scratch" that I did not quite know what to do with. Instead of filing it away somewhere, benefiting no one, I decided to organize and publish the material.

During my nine-year career working with children as a deputy probation counselor and deputy probation officer, I have been exposed to a variety of disturbing situations. I watch with a different perspective than most and notice patterns of behavioral problems displayed by our youth, stemming mostly from ineffective parenting. In my opinion, three basic principles could begin to repair society's sad state of affairs: respect, accountability, and deterrence (R.A.D). If these three components effectively worked within and outside of the home, what a wonderful place this would be!

Why does there appear to be such a lack of accountability, respect, and deterrence in our society? Friends and colleagues laughed as I passionately recounted my disappointment with human behavior and tried to change the world around me. How was it possible for me to make an impact on a case-by-case basis in my career and personal life? Then, a moment of clarity gave way to the idea of publishing my thoughts. Could my opinionated commentary bring about change, awareness, or a more selfless attitude in the masses?

Not everyone will agree with the thoughts presented in my book, but this process has been extremely therapeutic for me, and I am hopeful that my friends and family can laugh with me as I muddle through interpreting life, parenting, and human nature.

Chapter One

Moral Decay

Has anyone noticed the phenomenon occurring on our freeways? Nearly every day, vehicles cross the double yellow lines of the carpool lane. It is as if those lines do not exist at all. I find myself more and more angry with these individuals. Do they not know the law? Do they have an urgent situation? No, that is not it at all; they just do not care. They have no respect for the laws that govern our society or the nameless faces surrounding them. They seem to care only about their own needs and satisfying them without expending any effort, even if that means scamming, cheating, or stealing. They will do whatever is necessary to achieve the desired result. Sadly, these lawless, inconsiderate people are raising children who will likely display a similar disregard for others. Self-centeredness has taken over the masses. Where has this moral decay come from, and how pervasive is it? Judging from our freeways, the answer is clear. We face a major problem.

This decay has resulted in a blurred or skewed understanding of right and wrong. People are not born with morals and values. These concepts are learned, experienced, and engrained through years of practice. How can parents teach morals and values if their own understanding is skewed? Moreover, how can one teach morals and values when one's behavior contradicts them? Parenting skills have regressed to a state that impairs our youth. Even elementary concepts, like teaching children proper manners seem to be failing. Our youth know how to operate computers, program cellular phones, and "text-message" their friends, but do they respect their elders, excuse themselves from the dinner table, or respect authority? Our technological advances appear to have had a hand in retarding our ability to provide basic tools to our children. Is parenting a lost art?

The media presents us with a forum by which our children are supplied with negativity any time of the day or night. Public respect has waned for entities or individuals that debase civility for reward, yet the behavior is reinforced, instead of punished. Countless numbers of people become famous for scandal and exploit the situation for monetary gain. The media capitalizes on society's lust for scandal by sensationalizing shows, increasing the levels of blood, gore, or nudity for higher ratings. Even the news has become indecent, showing situations that are inappropriate for public viewing, but society is compelled to watch, and the cycle is perpetuated.

I love television as much as anyone does, but I have had to become more vigilant about the programs my children are allowed to watch. Even shows directed toward their age group are increasingly inappropriate. The biggest problem in today's world appears not to be the media or television itself, but the parent's inability to differentiate positive shows versus negative shows. Certainly, the media has greatly contributed to this inability, as it stems from being "desensitized." Then there is the age-old argument for "free speech." The type of speech we are encountering is not free; it is costing us immeasurably.

Basic behaviorism dictates that if unwanted behaviors are not reinforced by way of reward, the behaviors will decrease and become extinct. Yet, collectively, we continue to reward inappropriate behavior for entertainment value. Has entertainment preceded the standards by which we treat one another? If poor behavior were punished, rather than rewarded, would we enjoy a higher level of concern for one another and begin adhering to laws that maintain order and safety? Well, I know that if sharp pieces of metal were placed along the double yellow line on the freeway, I sure would not be crossing it!

Children being raised today are given a sense of independence at a young age, not fully understanding anyone's needs but their own. They are often given rights and privileges before they understand the concepts. Exacerbating this further is how parents empower children to challenge rules and authority instead of complying with them.

Many children are not required to earn privileges or carry out tasks that build responsibility, experience, patience, and character. This entitlement creates a lack of frustration tolerance, which results in atrocious coping skills. Inevitably, parents who set poor boundaries and low standards of behavior for their children encounter early behavioral problems. As the child grows in age, size, and intellect, he or she becomes increasingly difficult to control, supervise, and punish. Sadly, parents are often unsure what generated the lack of respect for their authority.

I regularly interview children as young as twelve as they explain, in detail, the crimes they have committed. In one memorable interview, a fourteen-year-old female recounted a gang-related stabbing in which she was involved. The victim was stabbed, chased, then stabbed some more as he tried to crawl to safety. The girl was completely cavalier. Not only was she unaffected by her incarceration, but even more alarming, she had no reaction of horror, regret, or even sadness over the violent death of a peer. She referred to the victim as a "fool" and felt he deserved to die. The girl was completely void of conscience. How does a child become so apathetic? These types of children are becoming more and more common and are extremely dangerous. Many believe children should be given leniency, chances, and be held to different standards, because after all, they are just innocent children. They obviously are far removed from the realities of the conscienceless child.

A child has a very short point of reference. They are unable to reflect on societal change. The moral standards and attitudes of society, however low, are normal, or acceptable, and thus internalized. If a parent does not supply a child with elevated standards for behavior, morals, and values, those lessons will be learned through society (television, peers, or others). Parents need to be active participants in their children's lives by modeling desired behaviors and ensuring others do not derail the lessons in the process.

This does not appear to be happening. More and more, parents are ill equipped and rely heavily on other adults (police officers, probation officers, day care/nannies, teachers, counselors, and relatives) to rear their children. Compounding this issue is the lack of social pressure that once helped dictate appropriate behaviors. People are absorbed in their own routines and oblivious to others. I think the most poignant example of this occurs when individuals talk on their cellular phones as they check out of the grocery store or order food. These individuals affect those they are supposed to be interfacing with and leave them with a sense of worthlessness.

It is a parent's responsibility to offset this lack of societal regard. Morals and values begin in the home. Take time to explain and demonstrate these concepts. Surround your family with those who share like values, and limit exposure to those who derail what you are attempting to accomplish. To teach morals and values properly, one should possess these traits and model them routinely. Evaluate your own morals. Is your interpretation black and white, or is there much gray area?

Parents need to get back to basics and begin to teach and model manners effectively. Perhaps the reason these basic lessons are not being learned stems from the simple fact that children model their parents' behavior, rather than doing as they say. They watch their parents' interactions with others and are keenly aware of tone and attitude. Are we behaving nicely? Do we become upset at other motorists and say angry things? Do we become impatient with others and behave discourteously? Do we interact with our spouse in a manner that promotes family harmony? Take an inventory of how you really behave, because your children imitate your behavior and take copious notes. On occasion, my four-year-old has brought attention to my negative behavior. I am always amazed with his astute observations. Children are like computers that store programmed information for later use. Make sure the information being stored is what you intended to program.

KEY CONCEPTS

- **BASIC BEHAVIORISM DICTATES THAT IF UNWANTED BEHAVIORS ARE NOT REINFORCED BY WAY OF REWARD, THE BEHAVIORS WILL DECREASE AND BECOME EXTINCT.**

- **HOW CAN COMMUNITY OR SOLIDARITY EXIST IF PEOPLE ARE INSULATED IN THEIR OWN INTERESTS?**

- **MANY CHILDREN ARE NOT REQUIRED TO EARN PRIVILEGES OR CARRY OUT TASKS THAT BUILD RESPONSIBILITY, EXPERIENCE, PATIENCE, AND CHARACTER.**

- **PARENTS WHO SET POOR BOUNDARIES AND LOW STANDARDS OF BEHAVIOR FOR THEIR CHILDREN ENCOUNTER EARLY BEHAVIORAL PROBLEMS.**

Chapter Two

Societal Changes That Shape Behavior

Within the last fifty years, significant events have shaped the world in which we live, and contributed to moral decay. The largest contributors include television, disintegration of the family unit and religion, drugs, and technology. To understand evolving family dynamics and the societal changes that ultimately effect parenting, these topics must be explored.

People often say, "We live in a different world today," and I think that is an accurate statement. It is different. It is a more violent, ugly place than it was fifty or even thirty years ago. For some time, scientists have been attempting to research the effects of television to determine whether it really does influence people to become more violent. I don't think I am necessarily a more violent individual, but I believe I have been desensitized to many circumstances and events. When I was a child, shows on daytime television didn't depict violence, inappropriate behavior, or nudity. Today, profane language is acceptable; it is not uncommon to hear "damn," "son of a bitch," "dumb ass," or "bastard"- even in animated form.

I am more sensitive to this problem since I have a two-year-old who mimics everything he hears. I never noticed inappropriate content on television until my two-year-old pointed it out to me! I am nearly oblivious to stress, gore, and violence on television. Television shows have had to become even more cutting edge, just to exceed society's already tolerant appetites. Reality shows were created to satiate our need to observe others in disgraceful, embarrassing, and even dangerous situations.

Criminals are usually not very intelligent. Television has provided them endless sources of deviant ideas. We can all remember individuals who credited a television show for their egregious behavior. Then, of course, focus is taken off the criminal and shifted to the show or song that inspired the behavior. Our society is full of people who want to hold others accountable for their own poor choices and behavior. Case in point—individuals who sue cigarette companies for their bad health, or fast food chains for making them fat. Soon, someone will sue a major television network for making him or her violent.

Individuals today are not held accountable by society. It is always someone else's fault. I like to refer to this phenomenon as DEVIA or "de-valued individual accountability." This behavior is actually rewarded, and it has created a litigious society. Until accountability becomes collectively valued, these problems will persist. Do your part as a parent. Teach your child accountability in the home. Do not make excuses for your child's behavior. Allow them to make mistakes and hold them culpable for their actions.

Another change affecting behavior is the disintegration of the family. This phenomenon lends itself to major dysfunction in our society. Sadly, there is a fifty-fifty chance that today's marriages will end in divorce. Not only does divorce have a negative impact on the control and supervision you can provide to your child, but there are also other obvious repercussions for the child, whose family dynamic is forever changed. Parental supervision and control are greatly impacted when couples are divorced or separated. Single parents have difficulty providing adequate supervision for their children. They are working, often struggling to make ends meet with a single income, and are exhausted and stressed.

I am a parent of two young boys and have a husband who shares household and childcare duties. I find the responsibility of child rearing tiring and frustrating *with* a partner. The days my husband is not home, I gain a new respect for single parents who meet this challenge daily. It takes an incredible amount of energy to supervise, set boundaries, and correct and model behavior. Having both parents in the home lends itself to control and power in numbers.

In addition to the disintegration of the family unit, religion seems to have vanished from many households. Practically all religions practice fundamentals that promote being a good person, doing the right thing, and treating others as you would like to be treated. Additionally, religion creates a level of individual and social pressure that dictates, or promotes the adherence of good treatment to others. The fact many families no longer worship on Sundays surely must have a negative impact. Further, the absence of religion deprives a child of the all-important concept of "community" that places of worship provide. This further bolsters the selfish ideals of our youth.

Another obvious contributor to the ugliness in today's world is the availability of illegal drugs. Drug popularity has changed through the decades, but has posed a problem for many years. In the 1960s, LSD was popular. In the 1970s, marijuana was the drug of choice. In the 1980s and 1990s, cocaine and crack cocaine represented the biggest problem. Today, synthetic narcotics are produced and distributed, posing additional dangers to the user.

Many of the juveniles I deal with struggle with addictions. Although drug popularity varies geographically, from my experience, the drug of choice for delinquent youth is methamphetamine. Methamphetamine, also known as "glass," "crystal," or "meth," is inexpensive and has effects similar to cocaine, but creates a longer lasting "high." It has devastating effects on the user and is extremely addictive. Methamphetamine addicts are often aggressive and desperate. Parents of methamphetamine users report that their child's personality and/or behavior undergo radical changes. A child who was once gregarious and charming may become paranoid and uncooperative.

Last, technology has been a major contributor in shaping societal behavior. I believe it has bred laziness and a complete lack of "frustration tolerance." Children are not required to carry out tasks that build patience. Everything is delivered to them so expeditiously that they are not afforded the experience of patience. Further, many parents appear anxious when they observe their child experiencing frustration, which only contributes to the problem. These parents interfere in an attempt to appease their children and alleviate their frustration, but in the process cheat them out of life experiences that build character and coping skills.

I believe building patience and "frustration tolerance" in my children is important. I purposely do not interfere when my children experience frustration. I encourage them by saying, "You can do it; I know you can do it," or by giving them verbal directions that will aid them in alleviating their frustration. I may say, "You might want to untie those shoes before you try to put them on." Allowing a child to experience and deal with frustration provides him with a dose of reality and a feeling of success and fulfillment when they overcome defeat.

If you think about it, your life experience is vastly different from that of a person twenty to thirty years younger. When I was a child, I didn't have a refrigerator that spewed my choice of crushed or whole ice cubes. I had blue trays that had to be diligently filled with water and placed in the freezer. Then I had to remove the ice from the tray and repeat this process for as long as I wanted ice. When I watched television, I had to move from where I sat to change the channel manually.

There were no special channels dedicated to children. We had channels 2 through 13, and at least four channels came in so fuzzy they were not worth watching. We did not have cable or satellite television. We did not own a VCR. I remember two pay networks — ON TV and SELECT TV—and our family couldn't afford them. I remember being excited to watch a television special that aired at the end of the week.

Children today don't experience anticipation that builds frustration tolerance. They simply pop one of their favorite movies into the DVD player. They don't even have to wait until the movie rewinds! Instantly, they feel gratified. Children experience expedited gratification in nearly every aspect of their lives. This technological streamlining might appear positive. However, it has created children who lack patience and who feel entitled. One reason Americans are wasteful, fat, and unable to control themselves is because they don't have to get up to change a channel or make their own ice-cubes!

Since many technological improvements came about during my adolescence, I appreciate these gadgets, which simplified and improved my quality of life. Our youth feel no such appreciation. It is no wonder the younger generation has been labeled "the Me generation." They do not understand the concept of earning things, either. As technological advances become increasingly affordable, we lavishly distribute cellular phones, computers, vehicles, and other non-necessities to our children. These advances have simplified our jobs as parents. Instead of teaching responsibility and accountability by telling a child to be home at six p.m., some parents circumvent this process by calling their child on their cellular phone. It is not uncommon to see children as young as ten with their own personal cellular phone!

As technology becomes more heavily relied upon, the problem will compound further. I recall interviewing several sets of parents who were assaulted after they attempted to take their child's computer or cellular phone away as a form of discipline. Just last week, I was reviewing the rules of conduct for a home supervision program with a set of parents. The judge had allowed their child to go home to await future court hearings if the child complied with the program. I informed the parent that the child could not have a beeper or cellular phone, to which the parent responded, "Oh, no, you will tell him that, right?" Children view these privileges as necessities and can even become violent when these mediums are threatened.

I received an email recently that really put things into perspective. I always knew life experience was different depending on one's age, but I didn't fully understand the extent of this phenomenon until I read this story by an unknown author:

One evening, a grandson was talking to his grandmother about current events.

The grandson asked his grandmother what she thought about the shootings at schools, the computer age, and just things in general.

The grandma replied, "Well, let me think a minute. I was born before television, penicillin, polio shots, frozen food, Xerox, contact lenses, Frisbees, and the pill. There was no radar, credit cards, laser beams, or ballpoint pens. Man had not invented panty hose, air-conditioners, dishwashers, or clothes dryers—the clothes were hung to dry in the fresh air. Man had not walked on the moon, and your grandfather and I got married first, and then lived together.

"Every family had a father and a mother. Until I was twenty-five, I called every man older than I "sir," and after I turned twenty-five, I still called policemen and every man with a title "sir." We were born before gay-rights, computer dating, dual careers, daycare centers, and group therapy. The Ten Commandments, good judgment, and common sense governed our lives. We were taught to know the difference between right and wrong and to stand up and take responsibility for our actions. Serving your country was a privilege; living in this country was a bigger privilege.

"We thought 'fast food' was what people ate during Lent. Having a 'meaningful relationship' meant getting along with your cousins. 'Draft dodgers' were people who closed their front doors when the evening breeze started. 'Time-sharing' meant time the family spent together in the evenings and on weekends. We'd never heard of FM radios, tape decks, CDs, electronic typewriters, yogurt, or guys wearing earrings. We listened to the big bands, Jack Benny, and the president's speeches on our radios, and I don't remember any kids blowing their brains out listening to Tommy Dorsey. The term 'making out' referred to how you did on your school exam.

"Pizza Hut, McDonalds, and instant coffee were unheard of. We had five & ten-cent stores where you could actually buy things for five and ten cents. Ice cream cones, phone calls, rides on a streetcar, and a cola were a nickel. If you didn't want to splurge, you could spend your nickel on enough stamps to mail a letter and two postcards. You could buy a new Chevy for $600.00, but who could afford one? Too bad, because gas was only 11 cents a gallon. In my days, 'grass' was mowed, 'coke' was a cold drink, 'pot' was something your mother cooked in, and 'rock music' was your grandmother's lullaby. 'AIDS' were helpers in the principal's office. 'Chip' meant a piece of wood. 'Hardware' was found in a hardware store, and 'software' wasn't even a word. We were the last generation to believe that a lady needed a husband to have a baby. No wonder people call us 'old and confused' and say there is a generation gap."

Remarkably, the end of the email revealed the woman's age: 58 years old.

KEY CONCEPTS

- **DEVIA= DEVALUED INDIVIDUAL ACCOUNTABILITY**

- **DON'T ENABLE OR MAKE EXCUSES FOR YOUR CHILDREN'S BEHAVIOR UNLESS YOU ARE WILLING TO DO SO FOR THE REST OF THEIR LIVES. ALLOW THEM TO MAKE MISTAKES AND BE CULPABLE FOR THEIR ACTIONS.**

- **HAVING BOTH PARENTS IN THE HOME LENDS ITSELF TO CONTROL AND POWER IN NUMBERS.**

- **CHILDREN VIEW PRIVILEGES AS NECESSITIES AND CAN EVEN BECOME VIOLENT WHEN THOSE PRIVILEGES ARE THREATENED.**

Chapter Three

R.A.D
Respect, Accountability, Deterrence

Now that we know what we are up against and have identified the environmental and social issues we have to contend with (which will inevitably interfere with our attempts to be effective parents) let's explore the concept of R.A.D.

Three important components must exist in a successful household:

1) *Respect*
2) *Accountability* and
3) *Deterrence.*

Respect refers to how a child views and responds to his parent's authority. I believe I should love, empathize, understand, and safeguard my child, but I do not have to respect my child's wishes or demands. If I did, I would be giving him candy for dinner and letting him play outside until eight p.m. So in this context, respect refers mostly to the level of respect a child holds for his parents.

A child of any age must respect his parents and their authority, or major problems will surface. I like to use an employee/ boss situation as an analogy. It is reflective of a child/parent situation within the home, and speaks volumes.

Most people have worked for someone for whom they felt little respect. Maybe the individual was incompetent, lacked scruples, or treated you badly. Despite the reason, usually your behavior was affected in several ways—not always in the following order:

First, your level of cooperation decreased. You became less willing to take initiative or comply with rules and direction. Second, your level of productivity decreased. Who wants to produce for someone whose praise and appreciation are virtually meaningless? Next, your attitude suffered. You developed disdain for the individual. Your attitude likely reflected the contempt you possessed and an outward show of disrespect surfaced. Last, if you had not already driven the person out, you probably felt like quitting the job altogether. You likely decided that working for someone for whom you had little respect made you feel worthless, unmotivated, and unhappy. In the end, you quit your job, and moved on.

With this analogy in mind, know that if your child does not respect you, cooperation, productivity, and attitude will suffer and "attrition" may occur. Attrition usually takes the form of running away or complete non-compliance. Children do not respect a weak parent, just as they do not respect a tyrannical parent. Certainly, many of us can reflect back to bosses who possessed these irritating traits. A child perceives a weak or tyrannical parent as either incompetent or unfair, just as you might in the workplace. Unfortunately, some parents find it difficult to maintain a happy medium between the two extremes, and their children's behavior suffers as a result.

It is easy to identify children who do not respect their parents. We have all witnessed a mother's humiliation when her child throws a tantrum and cries, "No," or "I want it," or "I hate you!" Children know that bad behavior in public tends to magnify or expedite the delivery of their desired result while rendering the already weary parent even more powerless.

Children who do not respect their parents may direct profanity at them, yell at them, deliberately disobey them, or defiantly tell them, "No!" These children are very uncooperative. They may be slow to follow directions or refuse to follow reasonable direction altogether.

They disregard re-direction or consequences and repeat problematic behaviors, unmotivated by the notion of consequence. Children who do not respect parental authority are far more apt to assault their parents. If they are allowed to do this once without being properly punished, it will become a difficult pattern to break.

An unbelievable number of juveniles are booked into juvenile hall for assaulting their parents. Ninety-nine percent of the time, it is not the first time they hit their parent(s). The parent usually has been assaulted numerous times and has either not involved authorities or not allowed their child to be arrested. These children don't just slap their parents or throw tantrums; they truly frighten their parents.

Countless parents tearfully recount their child's violent behavior in my office. Their child pulled their hair as they were driving. Their child held them down and punched them with closed fists. Once, I even interviewed a father whose lip had been partially bitten off by his son. Often, parents reveal that their child destroys household property or throws heavy objects at them. I routinely interview parents who inform me that their child has used weapons against them. And on the other side, I have interviewed parents who attempted to gain control by physically overpowering their child, only to be arrested for child abuse.

In one memorable interview, a mother began to cry when she told me how her son had been "terrorizing" the family. On one occasion, she had to lock herself in her bedroom with her two younger children, while her son issued threats through the door. The young perpetrator then cut the phone lines and tormented his mother through the night by repeatedly setting off the fire alarm. In another interview, a mother explained that family members had to hide after her son came into possession of a handgun and began shooting family portraits, yelling for them to come out. These examples sound like plots of horror movies, but they are some parents' realities.

If a child is willing to treat loved ones in this fashion, how might they treat their peers or authority figures, like teachers or police? How does a child's behavior escalate to such frightening levels?

Simply put, it begins with the absence of respect, accountability, and deterrence delivered consistently within the home.

Parents who are victims of physical violence perpetrated by their own children usually will finally contact authorities, but they let the problem persist too long, making it difficult to change their child's behavior. They assume that the police will intervene and counsel their child, and the assaults will stop. Unfortunately, this isn't the case for two main reasons. First, the consequence the child receives from law enforcement (usually a verbal warning, unless the parent desires prosecution) often does not deter the behavior. Second, the child possesses no respect for his parents or their authority.

Children understand that great offenses demand great consequences and obviously hitting a parent should be deemed a royal offense. Some parents make the mistake of minimizing the gravity of the offense by issuing an unsuitable consequence. If a child receives a warning or worse yet, numerous warnings for what he believes is a grand infraction, he naturally comes to believe the behavior must not be that bad. Why else would he receive virtually no consequence? Children do not deem certain behaviors unacceptable if they are not given a fitting or meaningful consequence. In other words, consequences that fit the crime are very important in laying the groundwork for a child's understanding of morals and right and wrong.

Often, a parent reinforces combative behavior by simply allowing it to continue. The child interprets this as, "This type of behavior is okay or tolerable." The parent further reinforces this message by providing little or no consequences, which skips the important deterrence step in "RAD." Children as young as one or two often experiment with boundaries; it is not uncommon for them to hit their parents. It is extremely important to have complete intolerance at the onset of this type of behavior, no matter what the child's age. The probability of a child repeating this behavior is then drastically reduced. If the behavior persists, increase or change the consequence to deter it. A loud, angry voice while giving very clear commands is often enough with young children. For example, "Don't ever hit your mommy again. Never!" If this boundary is not established when a child is very young, levels of parental respect will wane, and the probability of future assaults will increase.

Many parents make this critical error very early in the parenting game. They feel their child is too young to understand, and therefore, should not receive discipline. Do not make this mistake. Children are able to grasp cause and effect very well. Further, children may be unable to communicate verbally with you, but often understand every word. Test your child's level of comprehension; ask him to perform a task. My child may only know how to say a few words and is unable to communicate effectively with me, but if I ask him to bring Mommy his shoes or put his toy on the table, he is able to carry out the request easily. Children younger than one are even able to learn and use sign language before they can communicate verbally. Do not underestimate your child's capacity to grasp situations and understand your requests.

Accountability within the home is also extremely important. Children internalize right versus wrong through accountability. Children must take responsibility for their actions to learn and modify their behavior. Additionally, children need to understand why the behavior is wrong and feel regret and remorse.

If parents do not hold their children accountable, why should their children feel responsible for their actions? Many parents and/or children blame sources that are obviously not responsible, in an effort to deflect accountability and avoid consequence. After all, accountability is coupled with consequence. When individuals refuse to accept responsibility or accountability, they begin to believe they have done no wrong. If they have done no wrong, what incentive do they have to change their behavior?

Children need to understand why their behavior is wrong before they can feel regret or remorse. Explain why particular behaviors are wrong, even if the reasons seem obvious to you. Give examples to young children in simple terms that they understand. Often, all I have to do is ask my children, "Would you like someone to do that to you?" or "How do you think that made him/her feel?"

Regret and remorse enable an individual to internalize the behavior, making it an integral part of their belief system. Feelings of regret and remorse help develop empathy. When one internalizes a consequence and understands the effects their behavior has on another, a life lesson has been learned. The probability of negative behavior being repeated greatly diminishes. Additionally, the tools needed to interpret right and wrong are formed. Once accountability falls by the wayside, life lessons fail to become internalized. When a child does not experience accountability, not only do maladaptive behaviors become acceptable, but a skewed sense of right and wrong also becomes part of the child's belief system.

Consistently holding children accountable is a tiring process. Many times, exhausted parents ignore behaviors they know should be confronted. As a result, accountability suffers. Other parents attempt to provide accountability, but do so only intermittently. If you tell your child, "If you do that again, I will send you to your room," make sure you follow through with your threats. If you don't, you create your child's problematic behavior. The child will quickly catch on that you do not follow through with your threats. As a result, the child will repeat the behavior over and over to gain understanding of where the true boundaries lie. When a parent follows through, the child quickly comes to understand the established boundaries and tests the boundaries and parental authority less and less.

Unfortunately, some parents are fearful of confronting their child's behavior. They anticipate resistance in the form of defiance, hostility, or disruptive and embarrassing tantrums. The main reason these behaviors developed in the first place stems from parental inconsistency. The parent actually inadvertently trained his or her child this way by rewarding negative behavior unknowingly.

Take the example of a child who throws tantrums. We see it all the time. The child and his mother are at the park, and it is time to leave. The child throws himself on the ground and wails, "I don't want to go!" The parent then says, "We will stay just a little bit longer, then it's time to leave, okay?" This child has now learned the wrong way to get what he wants. The next trip to the park, if he would like to stay longer, he can throw himself on the ground and have it his way. These patterns seem harmless enough when a child is very young, but can become problematic months down the road when the parent is wondering, "Why does Johnny throw these tantrums?" Follow through is important. If you say it is time to leave, it is time to leave.

Two things can be done to reduce this type of problem. First, provide structure and set clear expectations for your child before you go to the park. Juvenile hall deputies use this method, called *structuring*, throughout the day, and it works wonders. Parents tend to react rather than explain expected behaviors beforehand, skipping a critical step. Children love routine; the unknown is a scary place. Explaining your expectations beforehand alleviates anxiety. The unknown becomes known, and your child's anxiety turns into confidence. For example, "Mommy is going to take you to the park! I expect you to play nicely with the other children and to share nicely. When it is time to leave the park, I do not want you to throw a fit. When I say it is time to leave, I want you to collect your sand toys and get in the stroller. Do you understand?"

A second way to minimize this problem is to give the child a warning that the time at the park is ending. For example, "Okay, it is almost time to leave; you may go down the slide three more times." Do not let your child talk you into more than three times. My four-year-old is infamous for this. He is always very cooperative, but he will try to talk me into four times down the slide instead of three. It seems harmless enough (really, four times is okay), but be forewarned, if you bargain with your child once, they will certainly try to barter with you in the future. Be cautious of using the concept of time (five minutes, ten minutes, etc.) to indicate end times. Young children do not understand "five minutes." This also acts as a cop out for parents who do not really mean five minutes. They actually mean, "Whenever you are ready, sweetie."

Deterrence is another important component within the home. If consequences did not exist in our society, it would mean, "Anything goes." It would be a lawless, scary place and certainly quite primitive. A *deterrent* is defined in Webster's Dictionary as something that prevents or discourages someone from a particular action, usually by way of fear or doubt.

Consequences we give our children act as deterrents. All children have to do is think back to the consequence they received in the past, and they feel discouraged from repeating the behavior. Often, the thought of the potential consequence acts as a deterrent. Even warning children of a possible consequence for negative behavior can act as an effective deterrent.

A healthy fear of consequence is what dictates my behavior and impulses. As a young child, I remember processing consequences and placing them in my memory bank for later use. Remember—a consequence that does not deter the behavior was likely not considered a consequence by the recipient. One of the most challenging jobs we have as parents is issuing meaningful consequences. A consequence must fit the objectionable behavior and provide deterrence. Then, most importantly, it must be closely monitored and consistently reinforced.

I often see parents make mistakes in this area, as well. The parent attempts to issue consequences for their child's behavior, but is not consistent. Sometimes they issue the consequence, and sometimes they do not. This creates confusion for the child and does not effectively deter the behavior. The problem behavior persists; in fact, it worsens. The parent becomes more and more frustrated. Why does Johnny disobey his curfew? The parent believes no consequence issued was effective, and they begin to get creative. They get desperate and start issuing bizarre, far removed, and sometimes hurtful consequences. For instance, parents who feel desperate enough to "kick" their child out of their home or parents who stop celebrating holidays or birthdays as a form of punishment. Most of the time, it was not the original consequence that failed to deter the undesirable behavior; it was the parent's inability to consistently enforce the rules they set forth. Once you set a rule, you must be prepared to uphold it. If you do not uphold the rules, your child will no longer perceive them as rules to follow.

Another helpful tip for providing deterrence is to explain "cause and effect" to your children. It helps them become better decision-makers. As a habit, I regularly ask my children, "What do you think might happen if you do that?" This helps them understand the effects of their behavior and allows them to practice decision-making, rather than having an outside source dictate their behavior. Often, they realize the effects their behavior might have and reconsider their actions. Many parents inform me that when their child is under their direct care and supervision, all is well. However, when the child is left unsupervised, he makes despicable decisions. As a parent, you will not always be there to supervise and intervene prior to your child making a decision they will regret. The goal is to teach your child good judgment and allow for practice, so your child is able to make good choices with confidence in your absence.

Consequences and communication must go hand in hand. Giving children consequences when they do not understand the meaning is purposeless. After you issue a consequence, talk to your child. Ensure they know why they are receiving the consequences and provide examples of what behavior is acceptable and expected in the future. For example, when my child throws a fit or tantrum because he wants something, I use a very stern voice and say, "I will give you nothing when you behave like that!" Usually, my child quickly stops the behavior because he knows this to be historically true. I then tell him, "That is not what you do when you want something. You need to say, 'May I please have a piece of candy?'"

Have your child repeat the desired phrase and give praise when they follow your direction. If I am not opposed to my child's request, I try to oblige after they change the manner in which they request the item, to show that using manners and respect will be rewarded, whereas placing demands and throwing tantrums will not.

Respect, accountability, and deterrence (R.A.D) are critical components in any household. Again, consistency in each area is paramount. If a healthy balance of each is exercised in the home, all members are happy and well adjusted. The respect enjoyed by the parent makes him feel at ease and under control. This in turn affects the child, giving him confidence in his parent's ability to safeguard him and keep matters under control. Accountability is the cornerstone that builds morals, which dictate right and wrong. When a child is held accountable, important life lessons are internalized, which ultimately leads to better decision-making and a more ethical life. Accountability also offers consistency when applied correctly, thereby adding to the stability offered by respect. Finally, deterrence provides parameters for behavior, as well as shaping positive behavioral patterns. When a child learns from his mistakes and makes positive life choices, he will enjoy a successful and stress-free life, as will his parents.

KEY CONCEPTS

- **A CHILD OF ANY AGE MUST RESPECT HIS PARENTS' AUTHORITY OR MAJOR PROBLEMS WILL SURFACE.**

- **CHILDREN UNDERSTAND THAT GREAT OFFENSES DEMAND GREAT CONSEQUENCES. GIVING CHILDREN A CONSEQUENCE THAT FITS THE CRIME IS VERY IMPORTANT IN LAYING THE GROUNDWORK FOR THEIR UNDERSTANDING OF MORALS AND CONCEPTS OF RIGHT AND WRONG.**

- **CHILDREN AS YOUNG AS ONE OR TWO EXPERIMENT WITH THEIR BOUNDARIES AND IT IS NOT UNCOMMON FOR THEM TO HIT THEIR PARENTS. IT IS EXTREMELY IMPORTANT TO HAVE AN APPROPRIATE REACTION AND AN ATTITUDE OF COMPLETE INTOLERANCE AT THE ONSET OF THIS TYPE OF BEHAVIOR.**

- **CHILDREN INTERNALIZE RIGHT AND WRONG THROUGH ACCOUNTABILITY.**

- **THE PROCESS OF FEELING REGRET AND REMORSE FOR YOUR ACTIONS ENABLES YOU TO**

INTERNALIZE BEHAVIOR AND MAKE IT AN INTEGRAL PART OF YOUR BELIEF SYSTEM.

- **WHEN A PARENT IS INCONSISTENT, THE CHILD NATURALLY REPEATS PROBLEMATIC BEHAVIORS TO GAIN AN UNDERSTANDING OF WHERE THE TRUE BOUNDARIES LIE.**

- **GIVING CHILDREN CONSEQUENCES WHEN THEY DO NOT UNDERSTAND THE MEANING IS PURPOSELESS. CONSEQUENCES AND COMMUNICATION MUST GO HAND IN HAND.**

- **MOST OF THE TIME, IT WAS NOT THE ORIGINAL CONSEQUENCE THAT FAILED TO DETER; IT WAS THE PARENTS' INABILITY TO CONSISTENTLY REINFORCE THE RULES.**

- **ONCE YOU SET A RULE, BE PREPARED TO UPHOLD IT.**

- **RESPECT, ACCOUNTABILITY, AND DETERRENCE ARE CRITICAL COMPONENTS IN ANY HOUSEHOLD. IF A HEALTHY BALANCE OF EACH IS EXERCISED, ALL MEMBERS OF THE FAMILY ARE HAPPY AND WELL ADJUSTED.**

Chapter Four

Parents

Many factors contribute to a child's unruly behavior. One of the most important and heavily weighted is the role of the parent. We all know that children make their own positive or negative choices that ultimately result in consequences, but these behaviors are related to their upbringing. There are isolated instances when an individual with a nurturing family and good upbringing finds himself involved in devious behavior, but generally, this is not the case.

In the many interviews I conducted, I have been able to identify ten types of maladaptive behaviors exhibited by parents that result in negative outcomes for the children they rear. Some parents will have one maladaptive parenting trait while others may have any combination of them. *Maladaptive behavior* refers to one's inability to promote one's own adaptation. I like to use this term to identify problematic behaviors exhibited by a parent or a child. Ultimately, maladaptive behavior in a child is behavior that a parent finds hard to deal with and invariably creates frustration and a lack of coping mechanisms for the child. Maladaptive parenting traits are those traits deemed ineffective and ultimately fail to promote a child's well being.

All of the parents I interviewed had a son or daughter who was arrested and brought into custody due to delinquent behavior. A large percentage of parents (approximately 85%) fall into one or more of the following ten categories. Parents who do not fall into one of these categories usually have a son or daughter who is abusing drugs or associating with negative peer influences despite parental re-direction. The categories are as follows:

1) The enabling parent
2) The buddy parent
3) The substance abusing parent
4) The absentee parent
5) The neglectful parent
6) The inconsistent/ineffective parent
7) The irresponsible parent
8) The spoiling parent
9) The negotiating/powerless parent
10) The despicable parent

The **enabling parent** makes excuses for his child's poor behavior. This creates a vicious cycle because the negative behavior has been validated and given purpose. Enabling parents cripple their children. They rarely hold their child accountable and actually perform tasks their child should be carrying out so they will not receive a consequence from another authority figure. For example, a parent might complete his child's schoolwork or chores so the child will not receive consequences from a teacher or the other parent. This parent believes there is a viable excuse for any negative behavior. If the child is doing poorly in school, it is because his teacher does not like him. If the child is disrespectful, it is because he had a bad day at school. The parent fosters and enables the child's poor behavior as he continues on a maladaptive path.

Some of the more extreme cases of enabling I have encountered in my line of work include parents who create alibis for their children to avoid consequence. This is not uncommon; parents will actually lie to law enforcement to protect their children. It is also not uncommon for parents to move their families out of the county to avoid apprehension or probation supervision. Enabling parents overprotect their children, sometimes even when they know their children are wrong. For example, many parents I have interviewed, especially from higher economic brackets, will assemble a team of lawyers to protect their child, who is obviously deserving of consequence. I find this particularly obnoxious. These parents question police actions, the victim's actions—any entity's actions—but rarely question their own child. Many times, a parent will vehemently argue his child's innocence without knowing all the facts. Then, when I inform the parent that their child has already admitted to the offense, they have no response and stare blankly, obviously shell-shocked. Do these parents really believe they are helping their children by insulating them from consequences?

Many of these individuals are well intentioned, but are unable to differentiate between love and discipline. They feel they will be perceived as "unloving" and find it painful to dole out consequences to their child. This is a very ineffective parenting style. Eventually, the child, instead of appreciating the love impeding the discipline, completely exploits the situation and uses guilt as a tool against his parent. Enabling parents are hung up on the way it makes them feel when they dole out consequences to their children.

The **buddy parent** refuses to assume a position of authority and truly believes that his child is his friend. This type of parent will engage in any number of juvenile activities. It is not uncommon for this parent to attend high school parties with the child or even provide alcohol to their child and their child's friends. Over time, the child becomes resentful and confused. He may like having the "cool" parent, but simultaneously, he feels he has no parent at all. This parent's immaturity is glaringly clear. Often, this type of parent will argue with his child as a sibling would and provides a very poor example.

The **absentee parent** spends more time away from the child than with him, resulting in complete non-parenting. This parent may work long hours or leave the child unattended for hours on end, requiring the child to make decisions that affect his safety and well-being. In extreme cases, this type of parent may abandon the child altogether, leading to foster care or group home situations. In the course of my job, I am required to contact parents after their child is arrested to advise them of the court process and supply them with important information. The amount of parents who do not even return my calls or attempt to track down their child's whereabouts if they have not received a telephone call from authorities amazes me. It is not uncommon for absentee parents to fail to follow up on their child's arrest. They do not know the whereabouts of their child, and often, they don't seem to care.

The **negligent parent** allows his child to live in appalling conditions. This parent does not provide necessities and allows the child to live in filthy, unsanitary conditions. These children often go hungry, unfed, and unbathed. Neglect can also take the form of emotionally absent parents. Some parents battle mental illnesses (depression, schizophrenia, bipolar, or obsessive-compulsive disorders) that render them incapable of providing for a child's emotional well-being.

The **inconsistent/ineffective parent** does not provide security to a child by instilling boundaries and/or consequences. This parent upholds rules only part of the time or fails to follow through. This parent does not give fitting consequences and fails to provide healthy boundaries. This type of parent might not set a curfew for the child, or may "forget" to uphold consequences previously issued, or give mixed messages (you are in big trouble, but you can go to the dance because that is important). These parents have good intentions. They love their children, but find the responsibility and effort of rearing them exhausting. Their children tend to be extremely manipulative and often dictate what behaviors they are allowed to exhibit. Children of inconsistent and/or ineffective parents avoid consequences for misbehaviors since their parent simply "forgets" to uphold them.

The **irresponsible parent** provides a less than comforting home environment. This type of parent may have numerous "friends" living in the home or may stay up late partying with others in the house. Worse yet, this type of parent may not have a stable residence, uprooting the family from motel to motel. This parent provides an unstable, inconsistent living arrangement for his children, constantly forcing them to adapt to yet another unhealthy situation. It is no wonder children in this environment act out. They have been unable to establish friends or support systems because of their transience. Further, their education falls by the wayside because their parents fail to enroll them in school. Included in this category are parents involved in criminal activity themselves. This type of parent engages in and organizes criminal behavior with their child in tow. Many times, I am unable to interview a parent because they were arrested for the same offense as the child. I have seen parents who have involved their children in elaborate thefts, drug running, and gang-related assaults.

The **spoiling parent** gives way to any whim or desire of the child. Once the child realizes he will get whatever he asks for, he exhibits extreme opposition to any resistance from his parent. "No" is not part of this child's vocabulary. This parent is not neglectful or abusive but quite the contrary. This parent does not provide consequences for their child's tantrums, combativeness, or lack of cooperation. This parent loses control of his child at an early age, making it difficult to correct the negative behavior in the future. These parents do not take into consideration what their child will be like several years down the road. The spoiled child has poor coping skills and a low frustration tolerance because he is used to getting what he wants. He simply is not fully prepared for life's realities because he is under the impression that his boundaries are limitless. Spoiled children catch on quickly that things operate differently in the outside world, but they continue to exploit their parent within the home—simply because they can.

The **negotiating/powerless parent** runs the household much like a democracy. At a very young age, the child realizes he has negotiating power. His vote counts. This parent is unable to set firm boundaries or rules and uses negotiation to insulate him from being the "rule setter" or "bad guy." This parent feels uneasy in a leadership role, allowing the child to dictate his own terms and wishes. As the child begins to understand the power he possesses, his level of cooperation declines. Eventually, the parent loses all control when the child realizes he even has the ability not to negotiate altogether.

The **despicable parent** is the type of parent who should never have been blessed with children. He appears indifferent towards his children and has so many personal problems that he is not even capable of loving and caring for others. He is verbally abusive, emotionally void, and shows little love or affection to his child.

After reviewing these maladaptive parenting models, it is no mystery why our children behave the way they do. It does not take a genius to realize that Johnny is a sociopath because his mother was completely unavailable to him, or that Judy is violent and promiscuous due to her mother's substance abuse.

Sometimes parents who exhibit these traits discover why their child is acting out, but by that point, it is too late. By then, the parent is desperately researching boot camps for his out of control teen, who has completely lost respect for parental authority. These are the people we see on talk shows entitled, "Help! My Teen Is Out of Control!"

If you are experiencing problems with your child's behavior, it is a good idea to take an inventory of your behavior as a parent. Are you unknowingly the stimulus for your child's poor behavior? Be honest with yourself. Do you fall into any of the categories of maladaptive parenting styles? If so, congratulations; you have identified a large portion of the problem. Now take steps to fix it! Talk to your child. Let him know you have identified a problem and intend to fix it immediately. If you are an enabling parent, let your child know that you will no longer be making any excuses for his behavior. Explain that you plan to help your child better understand accountability by providing consequences for poor choices and by not interfering with consequences issued from other sources. Formulate a plan with your child and explain that this process will help him to become a stronger individual. Then, most importantly, be prepared to be tested and to follow through with the strategy you just outlined.

If you are a parent of an incorrigible child between eleven and seventeen years of age and feel you do not fit in any maladaptive parenting category, in all likelihood, your child has met up with negative peer influences and is making poor choices despite your redirection. Your child might be abusing drugs. If you are a parent of a child younger than eleven years of age and do not fit into the above described categories, possibly the problem is medical. Seek a doctor's advice immediately.

People need to think carefully about the obligation of parenthood and then commit themselves to the challenge. Every person thinking about becoming a parent should consider taking parenting classes. The only model we can use to gauge our parenting behavior is that of our own parents, and many of us can remember poor choices they made. It takes practice to become a good parent. It is a learning process, just like anything else.

You would think there would be more resources available to ensure that we are the best parent(s) possible, but there aren't. Teenagers are giving birth to children at staggering rates, and social services cannot keep up with investigations of children in compromising home situations. We research pet adoptions more completely than we do child rearing.

What is also rather troubling is the type of available parenting advice. For parents who actually do research parenting strategies, what advice are they receiving? There is no scientific, foolproof way to raise a well-adjusted, successful child. Many people use trial and error or tips the professionals deem effective. I have read much with which I disagree, but many deem it worthy simply because a "professional" wrote it. Be very wary and selective with parenting advice and remember that each child is different. What works with one may not work with another.

The best advice I can offer to those who do not yet have children and want practice is to get a job working with children. The first job I had out of college was at a group home that housed severely emotionally disturbed youth. It was one of the most difficult jobs I have ever had. These children displayed despicable behavior. They destroyed property, assaulted each other and the staff, and were the most uncooperative individuals I have ever encountered. My first days on the job, I realized how unequipped I was. The kids were so unruly I often sat in shock, unable even to confront the behavior. Or worse, nervous laughter would set in. I soon realized that I wasn't confronting the behavior because I believed, "surely they already know what they are doing is wrong."

The reality is that children do not know a behavior is wrong unless they have been taught. Explanations must be given for mundane, simple concepts you believe are already understood. Further, explanations must begin at a very young age. The children I dealt with at this particular group home had never learned or internalized the basic principles of right and wrong, and were now no longer young children; they were fifteen years old. They operated at nearly primitive levels, both emotionally and morally, and conveniently were labeled with a diagnosis to explain away their incorrigible behavior.

One method can be employed—consistency. If a parent is consistent and follows through with action, it provides security and stability within the home. Consistency is one of the most critical aspects of successful parenting. A parent can love, nurture, and be a great role model, but may be completely ineffective due to a lack of consistency and discipline.

Sometimes it is hard to see the patterns of your own inconsistency. You believe you are consistent, but in reality you are not. A true sign of inconsistency is revealed when your child repeatedly asks for the same thing. He has learned to wear you down to get the desired "yes" response. If your child is relentless, continuing to make the same requests, even after you have told him "no," in all likelihood, you are not as consistent as you think. I find that if my child asks for something after I have already told him "no," the phrase "I already said no—do not ask again" helps tremendously. If my child continues to ask after I have said this, I explain what will happen if he asks again.

Child: "Mom, can I have some candy?"

Mother: "No, it is almost dinner time."

Child: "Mom, please can I have some of that candy?"

Mother: "I already said no—do not ask again."

Child: "I really want that candy, Mommy." (Notice this is a statement, rather than a question. Tricky little guy!)

Mother: "Honey, Mommy said no, and if you ask again, you are going to your room."

Many times, the tone of the no plays a large part in whether a child thinks you mean no. If the no sounds more like a maybe, the child will notice and continue to ask. Give clear commands that don't leave room for negotiation. Say no like you mean no. As a parent, you will be overwhelmed with an endless barrage of "Can I" requests. Sometimes, you will need time to think about the request. Don't feel like you have to say "yes" or "no" right away. Tell your child you will think about it and let him know later. The last thing you want to do is change your mind. If you change your mind often, you set yourself up to be worn down and your child will repeat requests until he gets the desired "yes" response. If your child sees that you changed your mind on a couple of occasions, what makes the next time any different?

Consistency must be present, both individually and with others who share in providing childcare. If you and your spouse have different views concerning child rearing, inevitably, there will be problems, not only with your child's behavior, but with your marriage, as well. Your child will detect dissension between you and your spouse. The child will become an opportunist and prey on the weaker parent. This will create marital strife and bigger problems that will interfere with raising your child.

Discuss your views about child rearing before you get married. After all, most people get married to start a family, not end one. A child must see his parents as a united front. Even if you disagree with your spouse's course of action, do not interfere unless your child's immediate safety is in jeopardy. Discuss the matter later in private and agree on an alternative should the situation arise in the future. You and your spouse will have differences of opinion. However, your child does not need to know this. If your opinions on child rearing are so different that a compromise will not solve the problem, marital strife will be an ongoing theme. Seek family counseling immediately.

Any individuals and/or entities offering supplemental childcare should also offer consistency, both individually and collaboratively with your philosophy. Communication is imperative with both your child and his caregivers to ensure that your methods are being carried out.

Today's child rearing experts appear overly concerned with the child's feelings and have in turn provided advice that disarms the parent of their authority. Suddenly the word "no" should be replaced with "That's not okay." Ironically, parents who avoid using the word "no" certainly don't have any qualms about their children telling them "no." I cringe when I hear a child tell his parent "No!" This is unacceptable. No parent should ever allow a child to reply "no" when he or she is requesting the child do something. With very young children, the phrase "Don't ever tell me 'no'; do it now" is an easy remedy. If this is consistently reinforced over time, a child learns that obedience is not optional, it is mandatory. Parents that do not establish mandatory cooperation early on will inevitably experience behavioral problems because the child lacks *respect* in the R.A.D. formula.

Some experts believe an abundance of choices should be provided to guard against damaging a child's self-esteem. This empowerment of choice is a disguise to gain the child's cooperation because the experts have stripped us of parental authority. Experts warn that under no circumstances should parents shame a child when he does something wrong. Remorse and shame are powerful and useful emotions. They are the building blocks for empathy, which build human "connectedness" and the conscience. These emotions are powerful deterrents and are simply not being fully experienced by our youth.

One important element of my job as a probation officer is to assess a child's level of remorse for their actions after they are arrested. Sometimes this is the deciding factor in determining whether a child remains in custody or is released. If a child shows no shame, remorse, or regret for his actions, a "red flag" goes up. If the child is not sorry for what he did, what will deter him from doing it again? If the child has learned nothing by the experience and does not understand the effects his behavior had on another human being, then there is a distinct possibility that the child will victimize someone else in the future.

Do these experts have children of their own? Do these new, improved child-rearing methods ring true of real life situations? Will my boss or landlord say, "That's not okay," or "Let me give you some choices. Would you like to pay your rent on the fifteenth or the thirtieth?" These new and improved child-rearing methods put the child in control, rather than the parent. Further, they do not exemplify the realities of life and will ultimately foster self-centered ideologies. I want my children to be prepared for life. Sugarcoating realities or catering to every choice they make will not serve them well in the future.

If you subscribe to methods that undermine your authority as a parent, that is your prerogative, but don't be surprised when your child either A) goes beyond your control or engages in behavior that jeopardizes him and others, or B) seeks authority elsewhere and thrives in an environment he deems safe—for example, juvenile hall.

You are in charge as the parent. If you do not perceive that you are in control, why should your child? Young children do not want to be responsible for decision-making. As a child gets older, naturally, you should increase the level of responsibility. However, allowing a very young child to dictate terms and make decisions others should be making for him is a big mistake.

KEY CONCEPTS

- **IF YOU ARE EXPERIENCING PROBLEMS WITH YOUR CHILD'S BEHAVIOR, TAKE AN INVENTORY OF YOUR BEHAVIOR. I'M NOT SUGGESTING YOU MAKE EXCUSES FOR YOUR CHILD'S BEHAVIOR, BUT ASK YOURSELF IF YOU ARE THE STIMULUS FOR YOUR CHILD'S POOR BEHAVIOR.**

- **CONSISTENCY CREATES STABILITY AND SECURITY WITHIN THE HOME AND IS ONE OF THE MOST CRITICAL CONCEPTS A PARENT MUST ADOPT, REGARDLESS OF A CHILD'S AGE.**

- **A PARENT CAN BE LOVING, NURTURING, AND A GREAT ROLE MODEL, BUT MAY BE A COMPLETELY**

INEFFECTIVE PARENT BECAUSE OF THEIR INCONSISTENCY.

- **A CHILD MUST VIEW THEIR PARENTS AS A UNITED FRONT. EVEN IF YOU DISAGREE WITH YOUR SPOUSE'S COURSE OF ACTION, DO NOT INTERFERE UNLESS YOUR CHILD'S IMMEDIATE SAFETY IS IN JEOPARDY.**

- **YOU AND YOUR SPOUSE WILL HAVE DIFFERENCES OF OPINION. HOWEVER, YOUR CHILD DOES NOT NEED TO KNOW THIS.**

- **INDIVIDUALS OR ENTITIES OFFERING SUPPLEMENTAL CHILDCARE SHOULD OFFER CONSISTENCY BOTH INDIVIDUALLY AND COLLABORATIVELY WITH YOUR PHILOSOPHY.**

- **YOU ARE IN CHARGE. IF YOU DO NOT PERCEIVE YOURSELF TO BE IN CONTROL, WHY SHOULD YOUR CHILD?**

- **YOUNG CHILDREN DO NOT WANT TO BE RESPONSIBLE FOR DECISION-MAKING. DO NOT ALLOW A YOUNG CHILD TO DICTATE TERMS OR MAKE DECISIONS THAT SHOULD BE MADE FOR THEM.**

Chapter Five

The Critical Years: Birth to Age Five

A parent's role in a child's life is critical from birth to age five. Boundaries, standards for behavior, and established consequences for non-compliance must be well intact by this time. What you teach your children during these critical years will form the groundwork that will enable them to determine right from wrong and set the standard for acceptable and unacceptable behavior. By this time, children should understand that when they are good, there are positive consequences, and when they are bad, there are negative consequences. A child's conscience develops early. Children are able to empathize and understand the effects of their behavior at an early age. Perhaps not as well as in later years, but the groundwork must be laid.

If a parent has not laid the groundwork, and these principles are not intact, the parent will see his child exhibit negative behavior more times than not. More importantly, the child's behavior will be resistant to modification. By the age of two or three, a child should have already learned it is not acceptable to throw sand in another child's face, or to hit, slap, or kick others. Most importantly, a child should know he is required to obey adults.

In my opinion, a healthy fear of consequence and the parent who distributes the consequence should be established by this age. Think about it; if children knew they would never receive a consequence for any type of misbehavior, what do you suppose their behavior would be like? An overwhelming majority would reply, "Terrible!" Consequences, both good and bad, are the elements that shape behavior. Without consequences, maladaptive behavior is fostered.

In the past, spanking children was an acceptable norm and provided children with a healthy fear. Today, spanking is not very popular; no doubt due to those self-proclaimed experts who warn this method will permanently scar our children. Children are simply not experiencing true deterrence. I received a few spankings in my day, and can safely say I am not traumatized. In fact, I'm happy I received those spankings and can wholeheartedly admit they were well deserved. I respected my parents and possessed a healthy fear of them and the consequences they issued. I have internalized past consequences, and I know these experiences deterred future poor decisions.

From the 1950s through the 1970s, parents could and actually did drop their children off at juvenile hall if they deemed them out of control, disrespectful, or truant. Today, this is certainly not an option. Juvenile hall admissions are stringently controlled, due to overpopulation. Felonies and violent misdemeanors are the only offenses deemed worthy of detention. What options to discipline are left for children who refuse to cooperate? What do parents do when they run out of options and have a completely uncooperative child residing in their home?

In my experience, parents acknowledge their child's behavior is problematic and beg for intervention, but wait far too long to seek help. Sadly, there are limited resources and services to render assistance by the time the problem becomes severe. Further, the child's parental respect has waned and "attrition" has occurred.

A perfect example of this dilemma occurred at juvenile hall a couple of years ago. A parent refused to take custody of her son on Easter Sunday after he was arrested for shoplifting. She claimed she needed formal assistance and court intervention to change her son's delinquent behavior. She was extremely frustrated because her son continually violated the law, but always seemed to go unpunished.

The mother stated that the police were initially unable to lodge her son at juvenile hall because he did not fit the booking criteria.

The police attempted to release her son back into her custody, but she refused to respond to the police station and informed officers that she was unable to control her son. Police officers contacted juvenile hall, and an exception was made to allow the booking of a non-violent misdemeanor case due to the fact that no adult was willing to take custody of the minor.

After the court proceedings, the mother came to my office in tears. She said the public defender had made her feel like a heartless, horrible mother after she reiterated her stance to have her son held at the facility. She faced countless obstacles in her efforts to seek out needed help for her son because of technicalities in the system, but her determination paid off, and her son finally received a meaningful consequence. He was placed on probation, which provided accountability and deterrence while providing the mother with a contact person who could personally assist her with her son's behavior. This example is common. Our system is reactive, rather than proactive, which places parents in a dilemma. Unfortunately, many parents are not as persistent as this courageous mother. They feel guilty about their child's incarceration. Even more difficult, while visiting their child in custody, they get to observe their child's desperate pleading. Many children guilt their parents into removing them from the situation. Even the strongest parents often change their stance on incarceration after visiting their child in custody.

Custody intake probation officers at juvenile hall field countless telephone calls from desperate parents searching for help and intervention. Unfortunately, these parents waited far too long identifying the problem and seeking out help. If they had been more proactive, they could have modified their child's behavior before it got out of control. The best advice for the reactive parent living with a completely uncooperative child is to document the child's behavior through police reports and involve school officials immediately. Since the parent can no longer control the child, many times, all that can be done is to wait until the child commits a crime worthy of detention to facilitate formal intervention. If the child engages in behaviors that endanger him or others and immediate intervention is necessary (for example, substance abuse, running away, prostitution, or gang activity), placement in a boarding school or facility specializing in behavior modification might be necessary.

Many parents sabotage themselves by failing to hold their children accountable, even when parents themselves are victims of their children's behavior. I have interviewed countless parents who are assaulted on a regular basis by their own child, yet they only involve the police after the problem develops into a pattern. Many times, lack of parental respect generated and/or fueled the physical abusiveness and it is not a pattern that developed over a week, or even months. It was engrained by years of reinforcement. Older children who assault their parents were likely young children who assaulted their parents, and the pattern of negative behavior was never addressed. How does a parent discipline a child who becomes combative and violent with him?

It is sometimes difficult to see your child face the consequences of misbehavior. After all, a parent's goal is to protect his child. However, protecting your children from consequences puts them at a huge disadvantage. They will not be provided life lessons critical to their development. This is not to say that parents should be ruthlessly inflexible in doling out consequences. Parents need to balance how, when, and what consequences are issued. Consequences need to be age-appropriate and must fit the offense. Effective and meaningful consequences, both positive and negative, enable children to make responsible choices for themselves.

Pop psychology has developed new and improved child-rearing techniques, "discovering" a diagnosis that now explains away bad behavior. Attention deficit disorder (ADD), oppositional defiance disorder (ODD), and one of my favorites, intermittent explosive disorder (IED), are a phenomenon creating a large population of youngsters dependent on medication. Did these disorders exist when our parents were growing up? Have we only been able to identify and diagnose these behaviors in the past twenty years? Perhaps our litigious, med-dispensing society has merely assigned a diagnosis for unacceptable behavior, thus making the behavior acceptable.

Although people have differences in chemical make-ups, and there may be individuals who benefit from medication, far too many of our children are afflicted by terrible behavioral problems. Why now, and not in the past? Have microwave ovens and pesticides altered our genetic makeup? Or has our technology enabled us to identify and correct, or more accurately, mask certain behaviors. These attention deficit problems and oppositional behavior issues can more accurately be described as UMD (untrained monkey disorder). If parents do not train their children, they will most certainly act like "wild monkeys in a zoo."

If parents believe a medication will change their child and make him more cooperative, they are missing the fact that medications merely mask the symptoms. Even more damaging, children are provided with a socially acceptable, widespread, foolproof excuse. I'm confident there are a number of children who would benefit from medication. But is it to the degree we see today, where doctors dispense medication to treat behavioral problems?

Many children who exhibit behavioral problems are a result of poor behavior shaping, but it is easy to see why a diagnosis is more comfortable for parents. If both of my children were afflicted with ADHD or ODD, it would be much easier to swallow if a doctor said, "Your children have a chemical imbalance, and medication might be helpful," instead of, "You have been an ineffective parent failing to provide boundaries and consequences for misbehavior, and this has resulted in your child's unruly behavior."

KEY CONCEPTS

- **THE PARENT'S ROLE IN A CHILD'S LIFE, FROM BIRTH TO AGE FIVE, IS CRITICAL. THE BOUNDARIES AND STANDARDS FOR BEHAVIOR ARE WELL INTACT BY THIS TIME.**

- **WITHOUT CONSEQUENCES, MALADAPTIVE BEHAVIOR IS FOSTERED.**

- **OLDER CHILDREN THAT ASSAULT THEIR PARENTS WERE LIKELY ONCE YOUNG CHILDREN WHO ASSAULTED THEIR PARENTS, AND THE PATTERN OF NEGATIVE BEHAVIOR WAS NEVER ADDRESSED EARLY ON.**

- **PROTECTING YOUR CHILDREN FROM CONSEQUENCES PUTS THEM AT A HUGE DISADVANTAGE. THEY WILL NOT BE PROVIDED LIFE LESSONS CRITICAL IN THEIR DEVELOPMENT.**

- **MANY CHILDREN WHO EXHIBIT BEHAVIORAL PROBLEMS ARE A RESULT OF POOR BEHAVIOR SHAPING BY THE PARENT, RATHER THAN SOME CHEMICAL MISFORTUNE.**

Chapter Six

A Scientific Glance at Behavior

Parents often rely on trial and error or imitate methods used by their own parents when raising their children. No wonder some individuals have difficulty. They may not possess adequate knowledge or experience. If the learning curve is two to four years, the child will likely already be exhibiting negative behaviors the parent has been reinforcing the whole time. Take a child who has learned to throw tantrums to get what he wants. The parent would rather not deal with the tantrum, so he gives the child whatever he wants. This cycle repeats itself, making the correlation between the tantrum and the desired object stronger and stronger. The child sees the relation and interprets it as, "If I do X (throw a tantrum), it will result in Y (getting what I want)."

There is one difference between reinforcement and punishment. Consequence in the form of reinforcement increases a behavior, while a consequence in the form of punishment decreases it. Consequences that give neither punishment nor reinforcement extinguish a behavior. Learning and applying this theory is easy. Identifying the reinforcement and punishment is trickier. Sometimes what we perceive to be a negative punishment is actually a reward to some children. For example, a child who acts out in the classroom knows it will result in his removal. The teacher believes she is issuing a consequence by removing the child from class, but the child may perceive it as a reward.

There are four scientific approaches that should be practiced within the home to shape a child's behavior: Positive reinforcement, negative reinforcement, positive punishment, and negative punishment. Some "experts tout solely one approach. For instance, they might subscribe to only using positive reinforcement and recommend "ignoring" bad behavior rather than punishing it. In my opinion, when one scientific approach is relied on too heavily, problems often arise. All methods should be used when raising a child to create a system that is not easily manipulated.

Positive reinforcement equates to "If I do something good, I will get something good." This method is effective, especially when it is combined with other types of reinforcement. Of course, all children need to be encouraged and given praise for positive behaviors, but be cautious not to overuse this approach, in effect creating a child that is reliant on rewards for behaviors that should be expected. Parents discover that when this method is overused, the reward loses its value. Instead of changing the reward system or using other reinforcement in combination with the existing one, they keep offering bigger rewards—"upping the ante." Another downfall of overusing positive reinforcement is that when no punishment is experienced, the deterrence in the R.A.D formula is missing! When a parent focuses only on rewarding positive behaviors and ignores negative ones, this provides no deterrence and fails to establish a healthy fear of consequences.

Parents who only utilize a positive reinforcement approach tend to shape their child's behavior similar to that of a performing seal. The child only performs the behavior when the reward is available. This can be frustrating to the parent who finds they are required to constantly dole out rewards for desired behavior or attitude. If the parent is not present, the child refuses to display the behavior. The system begins to feel a lot like bribery and often backfires. Additionally, if the child has not internalized the application of the desired behavior, he is simply performing tricks to receive a reward.

Negative reinforcement translates into "Something bad will be taken away, when a good behavior is exhibited." An example is a seatbelt buzzer that ceases to sound when the belt is put on. This method is used least often because the parent must supply the bad stimuli that will be stopped once the desired behavior is exhibited. A good example of this approach is when a mother stops the vehicle and only continues driving towards Disneyland when the children stop arguing. The mother supplies the bad stimuli by stopping the vehicle and this in turn produces an increase in the desired behavior.

Positive punishment translates into "If I do something bad, I will get something bad." Spanking is an example of positive punishment. Positive punishment, when applied correctly, is the most effective way to stop unwanted behavior. Timing is critical when employing this method. Additionally, the punishment must be sufficient to stop the behavior and be more valuable than the reward. Obviously, a parent would not want to rely on this system alone; doing so would mean constant spanking or hand slapping. However, for the most unwanted behaviors, this approach really provides distinction for a child. The child recognizes that when he lies, he receives a spanking; as opposed to when he forgets to do his chores, he simply does not receive his allowance. He can deduce from this that the parent deems lying a more serious infraction than failing to do chores. The level of consequence should correlate to the degree of the offense.

Negative punishment translates into "If I do something bad, something good will be taken from me." Many parents utilize this effective approach and take privileges away to shape behavior. However, this system, by itself, has downfalls. First, you must identify what meaningful privilege will be taken away. Then suppose you have already taken almost everything away. If the unwanted behavior remains, what will you take when there is nothing left?

This chapter is meant to provide parents with an understanding of how different methods of reinforcement and punishment shape behavior. Using one method too heavily creates problems. Use all of the methods to create a system of rewards and consequences that cannot be manipulated. Again, consistency is the key! Do not prohibit a particular behavior on Monday and allow it on Wednesday, as this sends mixed messages to your child and discredits you as a parent.

KEY CONCEPTS

- **CONSEQUENCES IN THE FORM OF REWARD (REINFORCEMENT) INCREASE BEHAVIOR, WHILE CONSEQEUNCES IN THE FORM OF PUNISHEMENT DECREASE BEHAVIOR.**

- **POSITIVE REINFORCEMENT = DO SOMETHING GOOD GET SOMETHING GOOD
(INCREASES BEHAVIOR)**

- **NEGATIVE REINFORCEMENT= SOMETHING BAD WILL BE TAKEN AWAY WHEN I DO SOMETHING GOOD
(INCREASES BEHAVIOR)**

- **POSITIVE PUNISHMENT= DO SOMETHING BAD GET SOMETHING BAD
(DECREASES BEHAVIOR)**

- **NEGATIVE PUNISHMENT= DO SOMETHING BAD SOMETHING GOOD IS TAKEN AWAY
(DECREASES BEHAVIOR)**

Chapter Seven

A Caution to the Permissive Parent

An alarming number of parents fail to establish proper boundaries, give very young children too many choices, and/or have difficulty confronting unwanted behaviors. As cruel as it sounds, I am often amused watching parents use the newest tool or idea adopted from some expert in a magazine. They simply noticed the problem after it was created, reinforced, and perpetuated. Simply put, by the time they noticed a problem had developed, it was too late.

Even though a one or two-year-old may not be able to talk, he understands almost every word said to him. Parents underestimate their child's capacity for comprehension and understanding. Their standards and expectations tend to be very low, and they excuse inappropriate behavior by believing their child does not understand or is too young to receive discipline.

This error results in unwanted behavioral problems at a very early age. By the time the child is three or four, the parent wonders why his child throws tantrums in stores, whines incessantly, or is uncooperative. The negative behavior has been reinforced during the formative years. The longer the unwanted behaviors are allowed to continue, the more resistant to change the child becomes. Identifying that a problem exists is the biggest part of the challenge for some parents. The child begins to train his parent because the parent adapts to the behaviors set forth by the child, rather than the other way around. Unfortunately, some parents become used to their child's behavior; it becomes the norm. When a parent comes to accept problematic behaviors, the cycle of enabling rears its ugly head. Unfortunately, the endless excuses these parents create will last long into their child's adulthood.

A simple solution exists. Practice proactive parenting. Don't let behaviors develop into problems. Don't wait to address the problem until after it has manifested into a full-fledged pattern. On a daily basis, I correct negative behaviors and reinforce positive behaviors exhibited by my children. In doing so, I encourage behaviors deemed acceptable and do not tolerate negative behaviors. It is exhausting, but mandatory.

Some parents identify their child's problem behavior and take steps to change the behavior without involving or notifying the child. This is an important step of the process. Confront the behavior by addressing it with the child. Engage the child and help him discover why the behavior is unacceptable. After you have identified the problem and had some discussion with the child, inform him that type of behavior will no longer be tolerated. Often, if the warning is accompanied by an explanation of the consequences the level of compliance increases. Then, most importantly, follow through with consequences for the problem behavior if it persists. Don't automatically offer rewards for every act of compliance. Children need to learn to follow parental direction without bribery. They need to cooperate on the foundation of respect, trust, and love. If too many rewards are given, it devalues the integrity of the reward system.

Many parents believe that if they have allowed something to occur for several months or longer, they can't change the rules. You are the boss, and you are in charge. You may instate new rules, change rules, and do whatever you like. As long as you consistently uphold the rules you set forth, they will be followed.

Recently, I noticed that a bad habit had developed in my home. I'm ashamed to say that my family got into a routine of watching television during dinnertime. It had become normal to talk over the television or worse—to watch television more than we interacted with each other! Though this had become an accepted part of the routine, I decided it should change immediately.

I told my children that the television would no longer be on during dinner; instead, we would listen to music. The first day, there was much opposition, and my children were unclear why television was allowed before and was now not. I gave a simple explanation, and that night, we all listened to classical music. The next day, my children lobbied again to have the television on during dinner. I reminded them of the rule change, and they hesitantly agreed. By the fifth night, my kids were enthusiastic about the new dinnertime activity and wanted the music on before dinner even started.

I was a little surprised at how quickly I was able to change the routine. I think this is where some parents go wrong. They, too, adapt to routines and feel powerless to change them. As a parent, be aware of how very adaptable children are. I have come to believe that it is actually the routine children desire, not necessarily the activity itself. Television during dinner was just part of the routine. They did not want to watch television, per se; they just wanted routine!

With this in mind, think of all of the positive routines you could set up to counteract the negative ones that develop innocently enough—usually with parental encouragement. Could it be that children who are attached to objects that offer security (blankets, pacifiers, toys) are attached to the notion of routine—not the object itself? Many children who are attached to certain objects are trained that the object is part of the routine.

My children have never been attached to security objects; perhaps this is because there is a huge sense of security derived from the provided routine instead. Daily and nightly routines have been established. For example, before bed, we change into pajamas, brush teeth, read books, and use the restroom. Once in bed, we sing the ABC song and say prayers. This routine lends feelings of security to my children without using objects or idols to accomplish the goal. Children simply crave and thrive on routine. Equally important, routine simplifies and organizes the parents' job while enhancing the degree of consistency delivered within the home.

Boundary setting is another important concept you will need to establish as a parent. Boundaries provide reference points or parameters for what behaviors are unacceptable or acceptable. Additionally, boundaries provide routine and predictability. If boundaries and routine are not established when a child is very young, behavioral problems will surface because the child does not receive enough parental guidance or boundaries for his behavior. Boundaries are often dictated by common sense and proper judgment. In my experience, parents who demonstrate low levels of common sense often have difficulty setting boundaries.

Very young children are helpless creatures. They rely on adults to supply physical, emotional, and psychological needs. Proper boundaries give a child security. With that in mind, imagine what it must feel like to have no boundaries. Young children do not want to be in charge. They want an adult in that capacity. When adults take a position of authority, children view them as "in charge." They are expected to keep matters under control. Children gravitate towards individuals in this capacity because it provides feelings of security and safety. Some parents feel mean when they institute rules. Do not make this mistake.

Providing discipline to a child accomplishes four important goals. First, it holds the child accountable. Accountability helps develop a child's belief system and his interpretation of right and wrong. Second, it provides deterrence and acts as a parameter for behavior. Third, it establishes the parent as the authority figure and lets the child know who is in charge. This leads to a sense of security and safety. Last, it provides the groundwork for what will later be the child's own self-discipline. Self-discipline is not a characteristic we are born with; I believe it is directly related to the discipline we receive during our childhood. Let's face it; if my mother had not disciplined me as a child and allowed me to eat whatever I pleased, often to gluttony, would I practice self-discipline with my eating habits or other issues later in life? I doubt it.

As a parent, I communicate my boundaries and confront intolerable behavior with the children I directly or indirectly supervise, even when their parents are present and fail to do so. This may be an unpopular decision, as some parents are offended by my interference. They feel I have no right or authority over their child. This type of parent is more concerned with the way my behavior makes them look rather than the benefit it is serving. I am thankful, rather than offended, if another adult observes my child doing something inappropriate and brings it to my attention. I am more concerned with correcting my child's behavior than being embarrassed about my supervision. No adult should stand idly by as a child engages in unacceptable or harmful behavior. Unfortunately, many adults feel it is not their place to confront children who do not belong to them and this further contributes to the low levels of societal accountability and deterrence perceived by our youth.

When I was a child, there existed a community approach to child rearing. I was confident that any adult in the vicinity would supervise and/or confront my behavior in the absence of my parents. I was sure to comply with re-direction, and hoped and prayed they would not tell my parents. My parents raised me to respect the authority of my elders. You do not see adults cooperating like this anymore, probably because some parents are too busy making excuses for their children. This lack of accountability has fostered unacceptable behavior from both the child and the parent, who allows unacceptable behavior to occur.

I observed a perfect example of this phenomenon a short time ago. Two small children were fighting over a toy. They screamed, playing tug-of-war with the object. A third child became involved, attempting to mediate the situation. She, too, began tugging on the toy. The mother of the third child removed her daughter and allowed the two other children to continue the struggle. This parent obviously felt it was not her place to take control of the situation. All children involved misunderstood her lack of involvement. The two children fighting over the toy deciphered it as, "You won't protect me, help me, or keep me safe." To the child that was led away, it meant that their parent "Could not help or stop the situation, or simply did not care." This lack of adult intervention and authority is sensed by our youth. Children are no longer taught to respect their elders anymore. Then again, if a child does not respect his own parent, why should they respect any other adult?

I observed this same troubling phenomenon at my child's school recently. It truly exemplifies the lack of adult authority exercised and in turn perceived by our youth: I was waiting outside of my son's kindergarten class when I observed one of his classmates hit another child with his backpack. I waited a moment to see if one of the ten adults standing in the vicinity were going to confront the situation and when no one did, I told the boy to stop the behavior and sit down to wait for his teacher. A short time later, the child again stood up and began verbally taunting and assaulting his classmate. This time I waited a few moments longer, to see if any parent felt in charge enough to take control of the situation. No parent came forward and I was again required to halt off the attack that had now escalated. After I confronted the child a parent came up to me and thanked me for stepping in to control the matter. She said, "You know, that boy does that every morning." The fact that not one of the ten adults standing in the area felt empowered with the authority to stop this activity, serves as an explanation to why our youth behave the way they do.

Respecting elders is not something that comes automatically to a child. Before entering school, many children believe they are required to obey only their parents. For example, a short time ago, my three-year-old was told by his uncle to come into the house. His reply was, "You are not my dad." He was quickly corrected, of course, and told that he would obey and respect all adults, but this exemplifies a young child's mentality. He didn't intend the comment to be disrespectful, but was simply stating the facts as he knew them. He truly felt that his uncle did not have authority over him. If you don't teach your child to respect other adults, it will not come automatically. You can teach your children to respect adults while still empowering them to say "no" to adults who may attempt to victimize them.

When I began working at juvenile hall, one of the cardinal rules during training was, "It's better to start out tough and ease up, than to start out too easy and try to get tough." This theory proved true repeatedly. Staff that could not uphold boundaries and rules had the most challenging shifts. On their watch, the kids would plan escapes, fights, and engage in rule violations. There was a low level of cooperation and respect for these staff members. When these staff members attempted to change their methods and get tough, they had no credibility and could not earn back the lost respect. Eventually, they realized the job just wasn't for them and resigned.

Parents do not have the option of resigning. Take charge. Set rules and boundaries to make your children feel safe. The more comfortable you become at providing consistent boundaries and discipline, the more successful your child will become. When the time arrives for your child to make his own decisions, you will have been a confident and competent role model who carried out leadership decisively. As it becomes apparent that your child requires a higher level of independence and responsibility, afford it to them. Do not become so controlling that you are unable to allow your children to make decisions and exercise their independence.

KEY CONCEPTS

- **PARENTS UNDERESTIMATE THEIR CHILD'S CAPACITY FOR UNDERSTANDING. THEIR STANDARDS FOR BEHAVIOR ARE LOW, AND THEY EXCUSE INAPPROPRIATE BEHAVIOR BY BELIEVING THEIR CHILD DOES NOT UNDERSTAND OR IS TOO YOUNG TO RECEIVE DISCIPLINE.**

- **IDENTIFYING THAT A PROBLEM EXISTS IS THE BIGGEST CHALLENGE FOR SOME PARENTS. IN ESSENCE, THE CHILD BEGINS TO TRAIN THEIR PARENT BECAUSE THE PARENT ADAPTS TO THE BEHAVIORS SET FORTH BY THE CHILD, RATHER THAN THE OTHER WAY AROUND.**

- **DON'T LET BEHAVIORS DEVELOP INTO PROBLEMS.**

- **DON'T AUTOMATICALLY OFFER REWARDS FOR EVERY ACT OF COMPLIANCE. CHILDREN NEED TO LEARN TO FOLLOW DIRECTION WITHOUT BEING BRIBED OR CONNED. IF TOO MANY REWARDS ARE GIVEN TO EXPECTED BEHAVIOR, IT DEVALUES THE INTEGRITY OF THE REWARD SYSTEM.**

- **IT'S BETTER TO START OUT TOUGH AND EASE UP, IF NECESSARY, THAN TO START OUT TOO EASY AND TRY TO GET TOUGH.**

- **PROPER BOUNDARIES ARE ONE OF THE MOST IMPORTANT CONCEPTS YOU WILL CARRY OUT AS A PARENT. THESE BOUNDARIES PROVIDE REFERENCE POINTS OR PARAMETERS FOR WHICH BEHAVIORS ARE UNACCEPTABLE OR ACCEPTABLE. ADDITIONALLY, BOUNDARIES PROVIDE ROUTINE AND PREDICTABILITY, WHICH AFFECT A CHILD'S FEELINGS OF SAFETY.**

- **IF BOUNDARIES AND STRUCTURE ARE NOT ESTABLISHED WHEN A CHILD IS VERY YOUNG, BEHAVIORAL PROBLEMS WILL SURFACE.**

Chapter Eight

To Spank or Not to Spank

Whether to spank or not to spank is a controversial topic, but one that is so important it deserves its own chapter. Society has attempted to streamline behavior, just as it has technology. As a result, many creative ways to deal with behavioral issues have been developed. Many of them are effective. However, some methods appear overly concerned with validating the child's feelings, rather than addressing more important issues, such as complying with parental direction. Parents have resorted to methods that undermine their own authority. It is not uncommon to see parents negotiating with their children to bring about behavioral change. A parent's expectations for behavior should be non-negotiable.

Our society has veered away from spanking, a critical error in my opinion. A spanking is the most feared consequence for a child. Many times, I was deterred from a certain behavior solely based on my fear of a spanking. If used sparingly, this is a very powerful deterrent. Obviously, one should practice good judgment with this form of discipline, and several variables should be considered. The hand should be the only means by which to administer the spanking. Belts, wooden spoons, hairbrushes, or other objects should not be used. Spankings do not need to be forceful and should not be intended to create a lot of pain. Also, other forms of discipline should be used in combination with spanking. Spanking needs to be age appropriate. You should not spank an older child or young adult. Lastly, spanking should be reserved for the worst of the worst offenses. This makes a distinction for the child about what is most serious and unacceptable.

A spanking is a memorable experience that a child can relate to a certain behavior. I was spanked as a child, and I can tell you to this day for what offenses. I received a spanking for lying and deliberately disobeying my parents. Do you think "time outs" will be remembered? Some parents need to impose ten per day. I really dislike the phrase "time out." Who is the time out really for? More importantly, when "time is in," does the child get to resume the bad behavior? Most of the time, this seems to be the case.

I have never uttered the phrase "time out" in my house. I do send my children to their room to halt offensive behavior and give them an opportunity to reflect. Juvenile hall deputies also use this type of consequence; it is called *behavioral room confinement* (BRC). This concept is effective if it is carried out properly. After a child is sent to his room, allow him time to reflect on his choices. Make sure your child understands that when he is sent to his room, he is to sit on his bed to think about his behavior. This is not a time to play or watch television.

After a reasonable period of time, allow the child to exit the room and ask if he knows why he was sent there in the first place (hopefully, he will know). Reiterate why he was sent to his room and explain what behavior is expected in the future. The parent or individual who issues room time should be the individual who counsels with the child afterward. For very young children, ages three to five, room time does not have to be lengthy—between five and ten minutes, sometimes longer—depending on the offense.

Some parents become overly consumed with the particulars detailed by the experts and fail to see the big picture. They believe they need an egg timer to carry out strategies properly, or they get caught up with the one minute per age ratio—age two equals two minutes room time, age three equals three minutes room time. Two or three minutes in a room hardly seems enough time to reflect. Additionally, if the child enters the room and becomes uncooperative or belligerent, a lengthier stay is obviously appropriate.

Some parents believe it is acceptable for their child to go to his room and proceed to destroy property, curse, and/or yell angry threats. Some experts may condone this type of behavior, excusing it as a child simply "expressing himself." I strongly disagree with this. If I send my child to his room, and he slams his door or begins to scream, he is quickly confronted and the behavior is not tolerated. I abruptly open the door, and with a raised voice say, "No! Stop that right now!" or "No! Don't ever slam this door!"

My younger child is very spirited. Once or twice, he has challenged me after I told him to go to his room. This type of challenge only has to occur once or twice if it is properly handled at the onset. Defiance is one of the biggest no-nos in my house, as it should be in any household. If your child tells you no, raise your voice and say, "Now!" as you lead them to their room. If they struggle with you, this is an excellent time to swat the child's behind as you continue to give verbal directions. If a child is allowed to deliberately disobey his parent once, it could lead to serious problems in the future. If your child is not required to do as you say, his behavior will quickly deteriorate, and you will ultimately be required to *make* him do as you say.

When children are young, it is physically possible to do this, but how will the parent handle the problem when his child is thirteen years old? The child will be much bigger, and his poor behavior will have been permitted far too long, making it much harder to control. Juvenile hall does not allow a child to choose whether he wants to obey. It is not a choice; often, no resistance surfaces because choice is not an option, and the child is keenly aware of that fact. Do not allow your child to choose not to obey you.

Over time, irrational or abusive parents have gone overboard with spanking, which has given it a bad rap. Used correctly, spanking is one of the most effective forms of discipline, but communication and spanking must go hand-in-hand. Communicate with the child afterward and explain why a spanking was given. When I ask my two-year-old why Mommy gave him a spanking, he is able to tell me every time, and the probability of that behavior being repeated drastically diminished. Even a mention of a spanking brings about swift action. I can nag and use positive reinforcement, but none of these methods brings about behavioral change as swiftly as the mention of a spanking.

Some parents fear spanking a child will teach them aggression. This does not appear to be the case. Older generations, which used spanking as a common form of discipline, have turned out well adjusted. Some experts argue that children who are spanked are damaged emotionally or even traumatized. I interview many juveniles in custody for assaulting their parents. They are not violent towards their parents because childhood spankings made them aggressive. In all likelihood, the lack of spanking contributed to the child's out-of-control behavior. I was spanked as a child and I would have never dreamed of hitting my parents. I had a healthy fear of consequences, which dictated my behavior. Mom and Dad, thanks for all the spankings. I'm a better person for them!

Every child is different. For some children, a disapproving stare or a raised voice will bring about swift compliance. Obviously, spanking would rarely be employed with this type of child. These children are fearful of consequence and desirous of their parent's approval. However, some children are willful and will push limits and test boundaries with little fear. A spanking for major no-nos may be the only effective deterrent.

Pay attention to how the consequence affects the child. Spanking children when it has little effect on them or their behavior is counterproductive. If the desired behaviors are not exhibited because of a spanking, and/or it provides little deterrence, there is no reason to employ this method of discipline. See if another method is more productive and be sure to maintain tight boundaries. Some children are simply more difficult than others. Don't allow this to act as an excuse. Demand cooperation from a difficult child just as you would a compliant one. Difficult or willful children respond better to those they respect and see as an authority. They will exploit those who do not take charge.

Many parents I have interviewed report that they have received consequences from law enforcement or social services for spanking as a form of discipline. Parents are even inhibited from spanking in public, fearful that someone will perceive it as abusive or inappropriate. I have interviewed countless parents who complain that their child threatens to contact the Child Abuse Hotline. It is not against the law to spank your child unless you leave injuries (swelling, bruising, lacerations, or redness).

Use good judgment when spanking. Spanking should not be used to assuage a parent's own feelings of frustration. Spanking must be administered properly in order for it to be effective. It should be used immediately after the unacceptable behavior. It should be used sparingly, and leave no injury or mark on the child. Spankings should also be age-appropriate. Prior to approximately two years old, the child may not be cognizant of the relationship between the behavior and the spanking, and physically they are very small. After age seven, spanking should cease, and reasoning should be the order of the day. Usually, parents find they need only dole out a couple of spankings in a child's earlier years and they act as huge deterrents for the rest of the child's life.

Young children should have no doubt that the parent is in absolute control. A household should not be run like a democracy. When dealing with young children, they do not know what is best for them, nor do they want to make decisions concerning their welfare. This does not mean you need to be inflexible or authoritarian. Authoritarian parents require absolute obedience, providing no individual freedom. This parenting style is ineffective because many times, the child rebels against what they see as an unjust tyranny. An *authoritative* parenting style should not be confused with an *authoritarian* style; it wields authority, but is not as rigid. Authoritative parenting offers choices, but the terms are dictated.

When children become young adults, a democratic household may become appropriate. Obviously, more responsibility, choices, and independence should be afforded to older children who have routinely practiced good judgment. The whole purpose of being a parent is to foster an environment that prepares the child for the day when he finally leaves the nest. Young adults must be skilled at decision-making, responsibility, practicing sound judgment, and most importantly, they must be autonomous enough to carry these skills out with confidence. If we constantly make our children's choices, are we preparing them for the future they inevitably face? Even if children have been taught right from wrong, will they be able to apply what they have learned?

I am tough on my kids. I don't put up with a lot of nonsense. Fussing, arguing, bad attitudes, and disrespect are not tolerated in my home and will swiftly end in room time or a swat on the behind. I expect a "please" and a "thank you" for a glass of juice and a snack. Demands are not fulfilled in my home, only respectful requests. My children's behavior and manners are being engrained. Thus far, it appears to be successfully carrying over to environments outside the home. I don't have to prompt my children to say "please" and "thank you" outside the home because they are used to practicing these manners within it.

However, I am as equally doting and playful as I am a disciplinarian. I crawl around on the ground, play, cuddle, kiss until my lips hurt, and even spoil periodically. If you do nothing but discipline all the time and do not provide the nurturing environment children need, it can be just as detrimental. My children know my love is unconditional because the discipline they receive never affects the amount or level of love they receive. Further, I use communication with discipline to explain to my children that I love them, even if I do not approve of their behavior.

Love your children. Show them in words, hugs and kisses, surprises, and your undivided attention. Establish a healthy balance of doting and discipline. Many parents overlook their child's bad behavior because their love interferes with the needed discipline. Love and discipline are two separate concepts, but they go hand-in-hand. If you are concerned your children might feel unloved when you provide discipline, talk to them about their (or, more accurately, *your*) feelings. Let them know you provide discipline because you care, want them to remain safe, and want them to be successful in life. You are at risk of becoming an unsuccessful parent if you do nothing but dote and provide no discipline. Parenting is a difficult balancing act.

One of the funniest and most memorable comments my father made to me when I was a young teenager was, "Amber, I would love you even if you were a hooker with crabs." Although many might laugh and believe this is one of the most unorthodox, dysfunctional comments a parent could make, it was pivotal and extremely meaningful to me. There was security in knowing that nothing would affect my father's love for me, and I felt a huge sense of relief. I did not question my father's love despite the discipline he provided. I was more fearful I would disappoint him. I could be a huge failure, and he would still love me. Explain to your children that you love them unconditionally, and you expect them to make mistakes. Explain that you provide discipline because you love them and want them to learn from their mistakes.

KEY CONCEPTS

- **DO NOT RESORT TO PARENTING STRATEGIES THAT UNDERMINE YOUR AUTHORITY.**

- **SPANKING SHOULD BE RESERVED FOR THE WORST OF THE WORST OFFENSES. THIS MAKES A DISTINCTION FOR A CHILD REGARDING WHAT IS DEEMED MOST SERIOUS AND UNACCEPTABLE.**

- **SPANKINGS DO NOT NEED TO BE FORCEFUL OR CREATE A LOT OF PAIN. COMMUNICATION AND SPANKING GO HAND AND HAND. ALWAYS EXPLAIN THE SPANKING AND PROVIDE EXPECTATIONS FOR FUTURE BEHAVIOR.**

- **SPANKING CHILDREN WHEN IT HAS LITTLE EFFECT ON THEM OR THEIR BEHAVIOR IS COUNTERPRODUCTIVE. IF THE DESIRED BEHAVIORS ARE NOT EXHIBITED BECAUSE OF A SPANKING, THERE IS NO REASON TO EMPLOY**

THIS METHOD OF DISCIPLINE. DO WHAT WORKS.

- **SOME CHILDREN ARE SIMPLY MORE DIFFICULT THAN OTHERS ARE. DON'T ALLOW THIS TO ACT AS AN EXCUSE.**

- **DIFFICULT OR WILLFUL CHILDREN RESPOND BETTER TO THOSE THEY RESPECT AND SEE IN A ROLE OF AUTHORITY. THEY WILL EXPLOIT THOSE WHO DO NOT TAKE CHARGE.**

- **SPANKING IS ONLY EFFECTIVE WHEN USED SPARINGLY.**

- **IT IS NOT AGAINST THE LAW TO SPANK YOUR CHILD UNLESS YOU LEAVE INJURIES (SWELLING, BRUISING, LACERATIONS, REDNESS). DO NOT SPANK YOUR CHILD WHEN YOU ARE ANGRY OR FRUSTRATED.**

- **YOU WILL BE AT RISK OF BECOMING AN UNSUCCESSFUL PARENT IF YOU DO NOTHING BUT LOVE, PROVIDING NO DISCIPLINE.**

Chapter Nine

Patterns and Predictors of Delinquency

Working with troubled youth and their families for nearly ten years has enabled me to identify problematic parenting styles that ultimately create undesirable behavioral patterns in children. It has also become increasingly easy to identify those warning signals and patterns that predict delinquent behavior in adolescents. Often times I am able to easily make an accurate prognosis of continued delinquency based on a child's past pattern of behavior, the level of criminal sophistication, and existing delinquency factors. Identifying behavioral problems with very young children is fairly easy and predictable. Behavioral problems are often times in the form of aggression, disrespect, noncompliance, or embarrassing tantrums. Older children may indeed exhibit some of the same obnoxious behavioral problems as younger children. However, older children are often presented with greater opportunity to make self-destructive decisions that may lead to delinquency.

Children exhibit warning signals that act as predictors of problems to come. The more in tune a parent is to his child's behavior, the more likely he will be able to identify these warning signals and take early action. The sooner a parent takes action, the better the prognosis for the child. Warning signals in older children include, but are not limited to the following: behavioral or academic problems in school, truancy, increased defiance within the home, substance abuse, altered or unpredictable moods, unsavory friends, a pattern of running away, theft, physical violence, and dishonesty.

Many children I interview at Juvenile Hall have problems in all areas mentioned. Most are attending continuation schools or are enrolled in an independent study program requiring them to attend school only a couple of hours per day or once a week. The lack of productive time at school only compounds the problem. It creates idle time for the child and inhibits proper supervision by the parent since the child is left at home to his own devices while the parent is at work.

Runaway patterns are sure indicators of delinquency and problems to come. Children who regularly leave home without permission, especially overnight, are also included in this category. I have interviewed many runaway children and have learned that often times, they run away for two main reasons, freedom from parental control and/or substance abuse. Juvenile prostitution is also a troubling trend and is on the rise. I am constantly amazed by the amount of teens booked into juvenile hall for prostitution. These ladies are as young as twelve years old, are almost always reported as runaways, and are actually traveling across state lines with pimps soliciting them.

Sadly, parents of runaways are often quite helpless. The best chance they have at finding their missing son or daughter is to look for them on their own after filing a missing person report with the local Police Department. Police officers are not out on the street looking for the missing; they simply have higher priorities. From my experience, if a child runs away from home once, the likelihood of their running away a second or third time greatly increases; often it becomes pattern like.

Parents should be especially aware of their child's choice of friends. These individuals will influence your child and create situations that place him in harm's way. Trust your instincts with this issue. If your child's friends seem like "bad news" they probably are. Be certain to communicate your feelings with your child and demand that they spend time with other friends who are more positive. In some cases, even insist that your child have no contact with the negative friend. Unfortunately, many parents I interview disapprove of their child's friends, yet they still allow their child to continue to associate with them. Many times these parents even allow negative peers into their home. As a parent, I will not hesitate to directly inform the friend I disapprove of, that they are not welcome in my home and I may even provide an explanation as to why.

Being an active participant in helping your very young child choose their friends will benefit them later in life. I express opposition to children who do not display good behavior, by telling my children, "I don't like you spending time with Johnny because he is disrespectful and does not obey his mommy." My children almost always agree and usually can provide a specific example of Johnny's past problematic behavior. Do not hesitate to use poor examples to your advantage. Many parents tend to ignore instances where they observe a child behaving badly in public for two main reasons. First, they hope by ignoring the behavior, their own children will not take notice, and in turn imitate the behavior. Second, they do not feel comfortable or polite drawing attention to the behavior in public. Next time, instead of ignoring the poor example when it is occurring, draw attention to it and express disgust. Inform your children if they ever copied that type of behavior, they would be in BIG trouble!

Another warning sign of possible delinquency includes altered or unpredictable moods, particularly aggression. Sometimes hormones can be the culprit, but other times an agitated state or severe shifts in mood can be indicators of substance abuse. If your child is losing weight and/or is exhibiting unusual behavior you should be alarmed. Take your child to the doctor immediately in order to rule out any medical problems and to have your child tested for illicit drug use. Become vigilant and more involved in your child's life. Begin looking through your child's room if you suspect drug use or illegal activity. If you do find drugs or weapons, call the police. Don't move the item. Leave it where you found it and request that the police respond in order to file a report.

Many parents may be vigilant about actively looking through their child's room, but may not know what to look for or how to identify what they have found. Leave it to the professionals and err on the side of caution. Then get educated by reading books or other materials that provide information on various types of drugs, how they are ingested, and their effects on the body. Additionally, become informed on what the paraphernalia looks like i.e.: glass pipes, bongs, spoons, weighing devices, and syringes. If you find drugs, paraphernalia, or any other illegal items in your child's room ensure your child understands that his behavior is illegal, dangerous, and intolerable. If you do not take swift action, your child will underestimate the severity of the situation and likely feel that you are not that serious about the issue.

Many parents have difficulty involving the police because they feel conflicted about "telling on their child" and risking their child's arrest. Once you begin enabling your children, they will expect you to insulate them from accountability and you begin a vicious cycle. The sooner formal intervention is brought about, the more likely your child will alter his behavior. If you are dealing with substance abuse issues, you will want to respond immediately and formally.

The problem I encounter with many sets of parents is that they fail to involve the police and their child's pattern of problematic behavior is never documented. When these same parents realize that their child's behavior has become beyond their control, they beg for intervention from probation, the police, school, or other agencies. Unfortunately, when parents fail to properly document illegal behavior, assistance tends to be delayed. What these parents see as the child's seventh infraction, will only be recognized as the first. Additionally, these parents will have the uncomfortable experience of explaining why they did not properly address these issues at the onset. In all honesty, when parents fail to take proper action, their credibility as a parent is in serious question.

Communicate with your child about substance abuse. Express your concerns and your attitude of no tolerance. Be aware that drug users are desperate and often times dishonest. If you discover that your child is abusing drugs, seek help, even if your child tells you that they don't have a problem or that they can or will stop. The sooner a parent can identify a substance abuse problem the better chances their child will have with regards to rehabilitation. I recently interviewed a mother who failed to confront and disallow her son from using marijuana because she used marijuana as a young adult. This is unacceptable. Do not send mixed messages as a parent. Despite your youthful indiscretions, send a message of "no tolerance" for any type of substance abuse.

Theft patterns can also indicate a possible substance abuse problem. Drugs are expensive and children often do not have the means to purchase them. Children might take household items to sell or they may steal money from their parent's purse or wallet. It is also not uncommon for drug users to steal from their own friends or acquaintances. Children may also steal for reasons not related to substance abuse. This is still considered a delinquency factor that could spell trouble in the future.

Good supervision is a critical aspect of parenting. If your children have belongings in their room you do not recognize buying, ask questions. If they repeatedly tell you, "A friend gave it to me", be skeptical and become more vigilant. I am not trying to suggest you should never trust you children, but certainly practice an adequate level of awareness. I interview many parents who are surprised to learn their child regularly steals without their knowledge. A parent's level of control and supervision over his child is directly related to delinquency. Poor parental supervision and control are the ingredients for disaster. Poor supervision creates ample opportunity for a child to get himself in trouble and then stay in trouble unnoticed.

The level of supervision some parents practice amazes me. In one memorable interview, I spoke with a sixteen year old who was selling drugs from his home. He had mass quantities of methamphetamine, marijuana, cash, and weighing instruments right in his room in a safe stored in the closet. The parents were horrified and had absolutely no idea that this was occurring. Do you know what your children have in their rooms?

Obviously, as a child grows in age and independence, the levels of supervision and control should be adjusted to the child's behavior and level of responsibility. If a child is earning straight "A" grades, has an after school job, has friends you approve of, and is involved in sports, the levels of supervision and control will likely be minimal. This child appears to be making good decisions and the level of parental control and supervision will be far less than they would be if this child was truant from school and associated with highly questionable friends.

Technological advances have now created an additional challenge for parents. The website "*myspace.com*" should raise a big "red flag" for parents. Unfortunately, parents are not routinely monitoring or supervising their children's activities on the computer. On one occasion, I learned that a minor in custody had a website where he posted pictures of himself posing with gang members. All or most of the subjects displayed hand gestures indicating their gang affiliation. I interviewed the mother and informed her of this information and she was puzzled, she had no idea that her son had a website. Also not uncommon, young girls will post provocative pictures of themselves on this website. Camera phones are another source of trouble. I have interviewed several juveniles arrested for taking nude pictures of their under-age girlfriend on their telephones. Being in possession of child pornography is a serious offense and parents should discuss this concern with their child.

Patterns of dishonesty are also warning signals. Children as young as four years old can differentiate between lying and telling the truth. Spend time educating your children at a young age about the importance of ALWAYS being honest. This type of life lesson is engrained and internalized at a young age. Do not lie to your children or make promises that can not be kept. Also, if you have a child between the ages of 7-11 who lies chronically and for no apparent reason or motivation, be alarmed and seek counseling. Usually younger children who chronically lie have deeper issues that will only grow more exacerbated during adolescence.

KEY CONCEPTS

- **CHILDREN EXHIBIT WARNING SIGNALS THAT ACT AS PREDICTORS OF PROBLEMS TO COME. THE MORE IN TUNE A PARENT IS TO HIS CHILD'S BEHAVIOR, THE MORE LIKELY HE WILL BE**

ABLE TO IDENTIFY THESE WARNING SIGNALS AND TAKE EARLY ACTION.

- **RUNAWAY PATTERNS ARE SURE INDICATORS OF DELINQUENCY.**

- **PARENTS SHOULD BE ESPECIALLY AWARE OF THEIR CHILD'S CHOICE OF FRIENDS AND EVEN DISALLOW ASSOCIATION WITH CERTAIN INDIVIDUALS THEY DEEM NEGATIVE.**

- **ALTERED OR UNPREDICTABLE MOODS AND THEFT PATTERNS CAN BE INDICATORS OF SUBSTANCE ABUSE.**

- **ONCE YOU BEGIN ENABLING YOUR CHILDREN, THEY WILL EXPECT YOU TO INSULATE THEM FROM ACCOUNTABILITY AND YOU BEGIN A VICIOUS CYCLE.**

- **POOR PARENTAL CONTROL AND SUPERVISION ARE THE INGREDIENTS FOR DISASTER.**

- **THE LEVEL OF CONTROL AND SUPERVISION OVER A CHILD IS DIRECTLY RELATED TO DELINQUENCY.**

Chapter Ten

The Proactive Parent

Parents can greatly increase the likelihood of successfully shaping their child's behavior if negative behavior is identified and steps are taken to modify the problem at its onset. The longer the behavior is allowed to occur, the more resistant it will be to change. Parents wait too long to take action, ultimately leading to feelings of frustration and helplessness.

If you allow your child to do virtually anything he pleases from birth to age five, problem behaviors will likely develop and will not be easy to change down the road. When you finally realize that your child's behavior is unacceptable and sometimes even embarrassing, it will be difficult to institute new rules to modify the unruly behavior. The child will likely feel confused and betrayed and this inconsistency leads to feelings of instability. The child will wonder why something he was able to do in the past is now deemed unacceptable.

Although I do not believe that very young children have the capacity to apply complex reasoning, they do have a highly developed ability to understand cause and effect. For instance, a child may learn, "If I scream while Mommy is on the phone, she will end the phone call." Or, "If I scream, cry, and throw myself on the ground, I will get what I want." Even a child as young as two has the seemingly innate ability to manipulate during the potty training process. It is not uncommon for a child to proclaim, "Pee, pee, pee, pee," and run to the toilet—not because he has to go to the bathroom, but to shift his parent's attention to him from a chore or undesirable activity. I am amazed at a child's ability to manipulate at such a young age.

Every time a child exhibits a negative behavior and receives the desired result, the parent has effectively reinforced the negative behavior.

Hence, there is a simple solution. When your child throws a tantrum or exhibits a negative behavior to get what he wants, don't give it to him! Instead, give him the opposite of his demands, or something he does not want, like a spanking or time in his room. Then, teach the child the proper way to ask for what he wants. "May I please have a piece of candy?" Have the child repeat the acceptable phrase. Tell your child he will not get what he wants when he behaves in an unacceptable manner.

When parents routinely give in to their children's demands, they begin to feel coerced and controlled, and often resort to bribery for cooperation. These are the parents you hear saying, "If you are a good shopper, Mommy will buy you some candy." The child will quickly become beyond the parent's control as the parent continues to reinforce negative behavior by complying with demands dictated by the child. Parents should not have to bribe children for their cooperation. Set your standards of behavior high and expect cooperation.

Reality television is now tackling the parenting issue, attempting to become the new "expert" on the subject. The families depicted in shows like *Nanny 911* and *SuperNanny* have one thing in common: reactive parenting styles. If parents simply corrected their children's behavioral problems as they arose and were more "proactive," they would not need to resort to televising their family dysfunction. These parents have no R.A.D. in their homes, and their children verge on animalistic. These shows depict children urinating everywhere but the bathroom toilet, spitting, punching, and kicking their parents and the nanny, harming their siblings, and behaving in the most inappropriate manner I have ever seen televised. The outcome is always the same—the nanny devises a reward and/or consequence system and ensures the parents consistently adhere to the plan. Then, magically, the child begins acting more like a human being than a Neanderthal.

Many times, the biggest challenge facing the nanny is getting the parents to acknowledge that there is a major problem with *their* behavior. These television shows are helpful to some viewers because they give parents nifty ideas on how to handle their children. However, my concern is that these shows do nothing more than desensitize families to extremely incorrigible behavior. The producers choose the most dysfunctional families with the most savage children for entertainment value. I believe the families depicted in these shows are not the norm, and no parent should use this low standard to judge their own parenting skills or their child's behavior.

The concept of proactive parenting applies to older children or teenagers, just as it does younger children. The sooner a problematic behavior is identified and acted upon, the better the odds of modifying the negative behavior. If parents are not involved in their child's activities, the problem might persist for months, or even years, without even being identified. I routinely interview parents who are completely unaware that their child chronically uses marijuana. Where have they been? Even if lack of education contributed to their ignorance, lack of involvement is the main issue.

Parents who do not want to violate their child's privacy also amaze me. I have interviewed a number of parents who even allow their child to have a lock on his door. Some parents would never dream of rummaging though drawers or dare read their child's diary under any circumstance. If this is your stance, that's fine, but do not be shocked when your child is using drugs or engaging in other negative activities without your knowledge. Privacy should be afforded to roommates, not children.

This doesn't mean I will be performing shakedowns on my child's room or violating their privacy as a regular practice; trust is important. However, my child will understand that at any time I believe it is necessary or prudent, I will feel free to nose around their room to ensure all is on the "up and up." Remember, your level of supervision is directly related to delinquency. Low levels of parental control and supervision are ingredients that lead to disaster.

Defiance in the home can be very frustrating for parents, and it comes in varying degrees. When parents are not proactive, they tend to react slowly to their child's negative behavior, or ignore it altogether, sending a message that it is tolerable. Problems are not brought to the forefront quickly. When a child behaves defiantly, and the behavior is not corrected, it escalates, creating a child with a higher degree of defiance. In essence, children who behave defiantly have been trained that way by the parent. This process takes years. Very young children who are beyond control eventually become older and bigger out-of-control children.

One parent may experience passive defiance while other parents may experience flagrant defiance because they delayed correcting the behavior. A child exhibiting passive defiance may simply fail to do what is asked, offering excuses like, "I forgot." This is typical of many teenagers. Although passive defiance is still not acceptable, as long as the child eventually complies with what is asked of him, I am not as concerned. Conversely, flagrantly defiant children will direct profanity at their parents or say, "I don't have to do what you tell me" and there is cause for serious concern for this type of defiance.

Parents of flagrantly defiant children lose control quickly once the child realizes that he cannot be made to do something. This type of child becomes even more challenging because he has mastered the art of manipulation and is no longer intimidated by his parents' sizes or ability to physically control him. Not only do these children fail to comply with reasonable parental direction, they refuse to abide by any effort made to consequence their behavior. If a child has this lack of respect for his parent's authority, it is usually congruent with his attitude towards other authority figures, including teachers, police officers, and other adults. These children are particularly frightening because they have no fear of consequence. They truly believe they can do as they please.

I once reviewed a police report that exemplified this type of child. A fifteen-year-old boy got involved in an argument with his mother, physically assaulted her, and then drove off in her vehicle without permission. Police units were dispatched and located the boy driving wildly through the streets, running red lights, and erratically changing lanes. The boy refused to yield to police officers and even displayed his middle finger out the window. The vehicle finally came to a stop, not because the boy's conscience nagged at him, but because the vehicle ran out of gas. Not surprisingly, the boy refused to respond to police direction to exit the vehicle.

Finally, he exited the vehicle, and in a last ditch effort to avoid or minimize his consequence, he fell to the ground, holding his stomach, acting as if he had a medical emergency. An ambulance took him to the hospital where he was medically cleared and the boy was eventually delivered to juvenile hall. A child who displays this level of disregard will be resistant to any type of authority; positive behavioral change will be very difficult to attain if he is not placed in a controlled environment.

Proactive parenting is critical in resolving problems before they become difficult to manage. Options become limited when dealing with situations that are already out of control. When a child's level of cooperation becomes non-existent, the parent must resort to "making" the child cooperate. With very young children, this is physically possible. However, the only way I have seen this done successfully in older children or teenagers is through formal court intervention, and sometimes even this does not deter the child. If the child is not caught violating the law and no formal court intervention is possible, the only options are to: 1) wait until the child breaks the law and is apprehended by the authorities, or 2) place the child in a twenty-four-hour facility specializing in behavioral problems. The latter option is very expensive and should be used as a last resort. However, I have seen many children make positive changes after being housed in these types of facilities. Usually, boarding schools advise parents that the behavioral modification process can take nearly one year. The child actually has to re-learn positive behavioral patterns and internalize the effects his behavior has on others.

A proactive parenting style is critical when dealing with substance abuse issues. If a parent does not recognize the signs of drug abuse, the child's immediate safety is in jeopardy. Sometimes the signs are obvious. If your child returns home smelling of marijuana and has changed friends, DO SOMETHING! Communicate your concerns, offer support, and guidance, dictate your expectations, and explain the consequences for non-compliance. Then, most importantly, follow through! Drug use is caustic. I have seen divorces, bankruptcies, and family dissolutions as parents attempt to help their child through drug addiction. Immediate detection is imperative. Think of it like a fire. If you smell smoke, investigate and extinguish the fire before it destroys the structure. If action is not taken swiftly, the structure will burn to the ground.

Parents do everything they can to help their drug-addicted child. However, in attempting to help, many parents enable their child's self-destructive behavior. The child realizes early on that he is able to run away, use drugs, and make promises he does not intend to carry out, and there will be virtually no consequences for his actions.

Often, there is only so much one can do for a drug-addicted individual, other than offer support and seek professional help. Sometimes the addict simply is not ready or willing to help himself, which is a sad situation. Your best chance is to prevent this situation altogether through proactive parenting. If the situation does become out of control and measures have been exhausted, I believe the best alternative is a private boarding school.

This option is ideal because it completely takes the child out of the problem environment and completely disallows parental enabling. The availability of drug buddies and drugs vanishes and twenty-four-hour supervision is provided. It is no longer the child's choice to help himself; he is forced to "get clean." I have seen great results in children attending these programs, but careful selection of the school is imperative. This is a difficult decision and a very expensive one. You, as a parent, will only have the opportunity to intervene while your child is under the age of eighteen. Once your child turns eighteen, they are legal adults. You will be unable to force your child to get help. If parents must choose between boarding school and their child's death, the choice is obvious.

KEY CONCEPTS

- **PARENTS WAIT TOO LONG TO TAKE ACTION, WHICH ULTIMATELY LEADS TO FRUSTRATION AND FEELINGS OF HELPLESSNESS.**

- **EVERY TIME A CHILD EXHIBITS A NEGATIVE BEHAVIOR AND RECEIVES THE DESIRED RESULT, THE PARENT EFFECTIVELY SHAPED AND REINFORCED THAT NEGATIVE BEHAVIOR. IF THIS IS CONSISTENTLY REINFORCED, OVER TIME, THE PARENT WILL LOSE CONTROL AND COOPERATION OF THEIR CHILD.**

- **SET YOUR STANDARDS OF BEHAVIOR HIGH AND EXPECT COOPERATION.**

- **BE A PROACTIVE PARENT.**

Chapter Eleven

Parental Awareness

In the past, juvenile hall was a temporary home for incorrigibles and truants. Not today. Teens are committing more violent crimes than ever before, and the sad reality is that our youth are amidst violent perpetrators with whom they come into contact daily, either at school or in their own neighborhoods.

Many people are surprised to learn that some of the children who populate juvenile hall have committed extremely violent crimes, such as murder, robbery, kidnapping, and rape. Over the last nine years, I no longer feel shock or horror to the particulars of these types of crimes; I am numb out of necessity. Only bizarre or truly horrifying offenses seem committed to memory. Sex offenses, animal torture, and crimes intending major injury to a victim are offenses that remain disturbing for me and take time to fade from memory.

One such case occurred recently. It involved a juvenile who tortured his household pet. This case truly exemplifies the level of ruthlessness our youth are capable of committing. The juvenile decided to get even with his sister for an argument by killing her small Maltese dog. He strangled the dog with a leash, wrapped a rubber band around the dog's nose, used a plastic baggie to suffocate the animal, and struck the dog with his fists. After several failed attempts to end the animal's life, he finally succeeded by smashing the dog's head repeatedly onto the floor.

According to FBI reports since 1991, the United States has experienced a drop in violent crimes. However, in 1994, more than 1.5

million delinquency cases were processed in juvenile courts, representing a 41% increase since 1985. (Butts, 1996) Even more troubling, according to data gathered by the Center for the Study of Prevention of Violence, researchers project that by the year 2010, juvenile arrest rates will more than double, due in part to the increased numbers of youth between the ages of ten and seventeen. (Elliot, 1994)

In addition, the female offending population is also on the rise. Countless females come to juvenile hall for crimes more vicious than their male counterparts' crimes. I have interviewed or supervised young women who have slit their own grandmother's throat, kidnapped the elderly, or stabbed and killed a peer from school. Girls are committing the same violent offenses as boys. When I began working at juvenile hall in 1997, two units were dedicated to housing approximately twenty-two girls each. Although this number has fluctuated, it is on the rise, and to date there are eighty-three females in custody in our facility alone.

Another area of concern is the juvenile sexual offender population. These juveniles commit heinous sex crimes against young children. I regularly see cases involving teenagers who forcibly rape and sodomize children under the age of five. There is little community awareness regarding juvenile sex offenders, but it is a disturbing reality. Most juvenile hall facilities have units dedicated to separately housing this population and providing specialized treatment. This population is the most predatory and most resistive to rehabilitation. Many sex offenders have been sexually molested themselves and will continue the pattern, victimizing and molesting other children.

While adult sex offenders are required to register as such at their local police department, alerting the authorities that a sex offender is living within their city limits, most juvenile offenders are not required to register! Megan's law requires that citizens have access to the names and proximity of adults who have committed sex crimes, but most juveniles are not included in this list. The public is not informed or aware of this fact. New legislation should be enacted to require juvenile sex offenders to register. Some states have enacted these types of laws; others have not.

Most juvenile sex offenders are given up to one year at juvenile hall and ordered to complete a sex offender program. They are not tracked and can later seal their juvenile record. The public will never have access to this critical information, and these juveniles could even obtain a job working with children. Some juvenile sex offenders are sent to the California Youth Authority, which is equivalent to a juvenile type prison. These juveniles are required to register as sex offenders; however, many are given local time and rehabilitation. How much access to your child could a juvenile sex offender have? Unsuspecting parents are wary of the middle-aged "pervert," when they should be particularly suspect of other children, who could just as easily lure and victimize their child, then receive little or no consequence for the crime.

These trends must be counteracted with changes in regards to the outcome of court adjudication and a "no-tolerance" attitude by the masses, especially judges who decide the consequences for these crimes. If teens are not deterred from exhibiting violent behavior, why not continue as violent adults? I strongly believe that huge portions of adults in prison were once incarcerated in a juvenile facility. Youthful offenders are not being effectively deterred because of inconsistencies in all areas of the system. There simply is not enough public awareness of this problem because juveniles are afforded confidentiality. There is no knowledge of the offender's identity or the consequences they receive for their behavior. The only time a juvenile's identity is learned is when the matter is filed in adult court. These teens will potentially stand trial as adults and receive "adult consequences." Juveniles who commit adult crimes do not receive consequences detailed by the penal code; they receive a watered-down version. It is not unusual for a juvenile who breaks into a home, assaults their parent, or steals a vehicle to spend only one or two weeks in custody.

While you cannot completely shield your children from the violence and ugliness in this world, you can educate them, give them tools, and provide enough supervision to ensure they choose their friends wisely. Too often, teens enter juvenile hall after being influenced by peers. These juveniles have told me that as their companion engaged in the illegal activity, they did not know what to do, were scared, were wrapped up in the moment, or did not want to look "uncool." As a result, they failed to make the right choice. They allowed the event to occur, participating directly or indirectly, resulting in their arrest. Well-adjusted children raised in a household offering, respect, accountability, and deterrence tend to have higher self-esteem and are more confident in making decisions. They are better equipped to deal with peer pressure.

Many parents attempt to sugarcoat the harsh realities of life. They feel uncomfortable giving their child the cold, hard facts and are more concerned with creating an image of innocence and goodwill than providing important safety information. This does not help the child when they are faced with difficult situations.

Parents also tend to veer away from discussing subjects they feel uncomfortable with, such as drugs, sex, and molestation. Talk to your children about their private parts, and let them know that those body parts are theirs and should only be touched by them or the doctor. Let them know that they should not touch anyone else's private parts. Some parents fail to set up proper sexual boundaries; obviously, being proactive in this area is imperative. It can prevent your child from being a victim, or even a perpetrator. Educate very young children about those who may try to victimize them. Let your children know that there are bad people in the world who may try to harm them, then give them tools to deal with these situations should they arise.

It is critical to role-play with your child to help them practice and understand situations that may arise in real life. With small children, "What if" scenarios are a fun and easy way to help them stay in practice. Change the scenarios to see if subtle differences change their understanding. For example, I asked my son if he would help a stranger find his dog. He said, "No way!" I then asked if he would help a lady find her kitty cat. My son said, "Oh, that's different; yes, I would help her." The more open your communication with your child, the more trust you will gain. The more your child trusts you, the more opportunity you will have to provide guidance as they grow into adolescence.

KEY CONCEPTS

- **AN ALARMING TREND OVER THE YEARS RELATES TO THE TYPES OF CRIMES BEING COMMITTED BY OUR YOUTH. THERE IS LITTLE PUBLIC AWARENESS REGARDING THIS ISSUE.**

- **OUR CHILDREN ARE EXPOSED TO A PEER GROUP THAT MAY BE VIOLENT PERPETRATORS.**

- **YOU CAN'T COMPLETELY SHIELD A CHILD FROM UGLINESS, BUT YOU CAN EDUCATE THEM, GIVE THEM TOOLS, AND PROVIDE ENOUGH SUPERVISION TO ENSURE THEY CHOOSE THEIR FRIENDS WISELY.**

- **IF TEENS ARE NOT DETERRED FROM VIOLENT BEHAVIOR, WHY WOULD THEY NOT LATER CONTINUE AS VIOLENT ADULTS?**

- **MANY JUVENILE SEX OFFENDERS ARE NOT REQUIRED TO REGISTER AS SEX OFFENDERS IN SOME STATES, INCLUDING CALIFORNIA.**

- **UNSUSPECTING PARENTS ARE WARY OF THE MIDDLE-AGED PERVERT, BUT THEY SHOULD ALSO BE SUSPECT OF CHILDREN WHO COULD JUST AS EASILY LURE AND MOLEST THEIR CHILD—THEN RECEIVE LITTLE OR NO CONSEQUENCE FOR THE CRIME.**

- **GIVE YOUR CHILDREN "WHAT IF" SCENARIOS TO HELP THEM PRACTICE DECISION MAKING.**

Chapter Twelve

The Absence of Societal Pressure

When large groups of people cry out, awareness and positive societal change often take place. A community's response to specific issues also dictates laws and political climate. Unfortunately, there is not enough awareness of juvenile crime and punishment. Cases involving juveniles are not publicized, and when they are, the identity of the juvenile remains anonymous. The juvenile offender never is held accountable by society.

Society seems to think that juvenile offenders are rare and less dangerous than adult offenders. In my opinion, juvenile offenders are more dangerous because they are not equipped with years of lessons in morality or empathy. They lack impulse control and cannot foresee the long-term effects of their behavior. We all remember how invincible we once felt as children. Now apply that self-absorbed view to the concern they likely feel for others affected by their behavior.

A community's objective should be to rehabilitate juvenile offenders into law-abiding citizens. Many times, juveniles receive a slap on the hand for offenses that would be deemed serious in adult court. It is not unusual for juvenile offenders to receive little or no consequences for felony offenses. Additionally, consequences are not timely. I have seen consequences delayed for as long as eight months after the offense was committed—sometimes longer!

Consequences must be immediate to be effective. Would you hit your dog with a newspaper a week after it urinated on the carpet? How can one expect a teenager, or anyone, for that matter, to associate a consequence with an offense after such a time lapse? Waiting this long for a consequence only allows juveniles to manipulate the situation, instead of forcing them to face their actions and begin feeling remorse.

Furthermore, the consequences given to juveniles often do not fit the crime and do little to deter future delinquent behavior. The goal of these consequences is to rehabilitate and flood the offender with as many resources and services as possible to aid him in making better choices, but at what point does this effort become enabling behavior? How many times will we allow juveniles to offend before issuing a consequence that truly offers deterrence?

Ill-fitting consequences are not as uncommon as one would think. I recall a sixteen-year-old ordered released from custody to house arrest after he burglarized three homes. On another occasion, a seventeen-year-old gang member was granted another chance, despite the fact he was on his tenth separate crime. A short time ago, a boy was brought to juvenile hall on an outstanding warrant. He had been involved in a hit and run accident resulting in injury while operating a stolen vehicle, and failed to attend court. The juvenile was finally located and arrested; however, he was released from custody after one day. This offender's crime was de-valued, and its seriousness was made laughable. Communities would be outraged if they knew how little consequence some juvenile offenders actually receive.

In my experience, those who receive the most chances and leniency, despite their age, end up being the worst perpetrators. Their behavior has been adapted and shaped by a lack of accountability, and they will continue to repeat negative patterns of behavior without fear of consequence. When they finally come to the end of the road, they are incredulous, confused as to why they are not being given one more chance! Every individual or entity that did not provide accountability or deterrence, including parents, teachers, judges, and probation officers handicapped and placed these offenders at a huge disadvantage.

Juvenile court judges ultimately decide the consequences of cases. They hold enormous power, as there is no jury in juvenile court proceedings. These judges are not voted into office; they are selected without the public's approval or knowledge. Although many judges are fair and offer an adequate level of deterrence and accountability, some have difficulty being the "bad guy." They have good intentions, and no doubt have the child's best interests at heart, but sometimes fall short because they become emotionally involved, feeling sorry for the offender. They enable poor behavior by excusing it, granting leniency, or failing to provide deterrence through a meaningful consequence.

Perhaps more awareness and careful selection of these individuals are in order. We need judges who are going to hold offenders accountable, and not give individuals chance after chance to change their behavior. This enabling reinforces negative patterns of behavior, much like an ineffective parent. Furthermore, juvenile offenders are put at a disadvantage, in that they don't seem to realize that the same type of crime by adult standards actually holds a stiff penalty. They are used to receiving the watered-down juvenile consequence, rather than what is actually prescribed by law, and when they turn eighteen, many experience a rude awakening. Coddling youthful offenders does not rehabilitate; it sets the groundwork for failure.

How a society deems criminal behavior greatly affects moral standing and acceptable consequences. Compare the attitudes regarding criminals in America versus Japan, Singapore, or Mexico. In Singapore, consequences are severe, yet citizens enjoy a virtually crime-free society.

In 1994, an American teenager pled guilty to vandalism charges in Singapore and was sentenced to four months in jail, a $2,200.00 fine, and six strokes of a cane. There was a public outcry in America opposing the "barbaric consequence" being imposed. The story made headlines worldwide, especially after President Clinton asked the Singapore government to waive the caning. Out of respect for the president, the Singapore government reduced the penalty to four strokes of the cane, rather than six. The same day this was decided, the sentence was imposed. The teenager was stripped naked and fastened to an H-shaped trestle by straps. The caner then wound up, and using his full body weight, struck him four times with a 13mm thick rattan rod, which had been soaked in water overnight to prevent it from splitting.

Singapore responded to the objections of the American people by replying, "Unlike some other societies which may tolerate acts of vandalism, Singapore has its own standards of social order as reflected in our laws. It is because of our tough laws against anti-social crimes that we are able to keep Singapore orderly and relatively crime-free." Another Singapore patriarch, Lee Kuan Yew, stated, "The U.S government, the U.S senate, and the U.S media took the opportunity to ridicule us, saying the sentence was too severe. The U.S does not restrain or punish individuals; that is why the whole country is in chaos. American society is the richest and most prosperous in the world, but it is hardly safe and peaceful."

Walter Woon, an associate professor of law at the National University of Singapore also commented on the teenager and his family stating, "His mother and father have no sense of shame. Do they not feel any shame for not having brought him up properly to respect other people's property? Instead, they consider themselves the victims." Woon went on to say, "No matter how harsh your punishments, you're not going to have an orderly society unless the culture is in favor of order. Britain and America seem to have lost the feeling that people are responsible for their own behavior. Here, there is still a sense of personal responsibility. If you do something against the law, you bring shame not only to yourself, but to your family." My response to this is, "Amen, Mr. Woon!"

In Japan, members of society ostracize criminals long after they have been punished, and it is not uncommon for families to disown their kin based on their criminal behavior. In another example, inmates in Mexican jails used to be lucky if they were fed; family members were relied upon to provide their necessities. In America, our inmates are fed better than our military. What a disgrace! It is no wonder we have the crime rate we do. It's no wonder people become "institutionalized." Who wouldn't want to be a criminal? After all, criminals are provided food, education, entertainment, housing, and dental and medical care.

Britain also over-indulges the criminal and it is not uncommon for a number of juveniles in custody to receive the taxpayer's money to buy themselves birthday presents; others are sent on holiday as part of their therapy. Don't be so surprised; it is not uncommon for juvenile facilities in the U.S to send convicted juvenile sex offenders to professional baseball or hockey games to enjoy hot dogs and popcorn. This does not seem to fit the definition or purpose of rehabilitation and surely, the unenlightened public would also disapprove.

The social pressures in America that once helped curb unacceptable behavior seems non-existent, and our standards have been whittled down to a disgraceful low. Those who victimize others are tolerated and given numerous chances. They are afforded probation for the third time, rehabilitation, community service, and a variety of other services to aid them in making better decisions, yet they continue to make the same poor choices.

America needs to deem anti-social behavior and crime intolerable and disgraceful. Until then, I suspect we will make little progress. Americans put up more of a fight over cigarette smoking than crime. There are television commercials rebuffing smoking and there are virtually no public places to smoke in certain communities, not even at a beach or the park near my home. America's choice of battles amuses me. I feel sorry for smokers, and I do not smoke. Why are we not collectively more concerned about those who are really victimizing others? Why have we not rebuffed criminals or those who terrorize our own streets? Until the moral climate of America shifts and a no tolerance stance for criminality becomes the accepted norm, we will continue to face this problem.

KEY CONCEPTS

- **CONSEQUENCES MUST BE IMMEDIATE TO BE EFFECTIVE.**

- **CODDLING YOUTHFUL OFFENDERS AND GIVING COUNTLESS CHANCES DOES NOT REHABILITATE; IT SETS THE GROUNDWORK FOR FAILURE.**

- **CONSEQUENCES MUST DETER BEHAVIOR TO BE EFFECTIVE.**

- **WHY HAVE WE NOT COLLECTIVELY REBUFFED CRIMINALS?**

- **THE SOCIAL PRESSURES IN AMERICA THAT ONCE HELPED CURB UNACCEPTABLE BEHAVIOR SEEM NON-EXISTENT AND OUR STANDARDS HAVE BEEN WHITTLED DOWN TO A DISGRACEFUL LOW.**

Chapter Thirteen

The Solution

I am continually surprised by human behavior. Last week, I was at a shopping mall, eating lunch in a food court, when I observed two children no older than four years old running to claim a table without any parental supervision. I thought it odd that a parent would allow such small children to be left unsupervised; clearly, the cashier was too far from the tables. I continued to eat, then saw one of the young boys jump on top of the table, wild-eyed, and begin dancing and hollering. I was astonished and speechless that a child this young would have the courage to engage in such a mannerless act. I wondered, "Does this child do this at home?" I waited, expecting a parent to come at any moment to publicly scold the child. Not only did no such parent arrive, but others nearby ignored the behavior, feeling powerless to take control of the situation.

As the child reveled in his wild behavior, my son was taking copious notes in his mind. This boy had to be stopped. I stood up and yelled, "Little boy, you sit down right now!" He immediately complied and appeared shell-shocked that someone was providing firm boundaries. He sat there another five minutes carefully watching me, obviously feeling scared. His mother finally arrived with the food and proclaimed, "Look at my two little angels!"

These days, if a parent dares to point out someone else's child's negative behavior, it is likely met with hostility. Usually, this is not a deterrent for me, but I was feeling particularly tired that day. It is unfortunate that parents have difficulty accepting criticism. They know, deep down, that their child's behavior is a direct reflection of their own faulty parenting. These same parents will be the ones asking themselves what went wrong ten years down the road as they search for help and welcome advice from strangers. Sadly, by that point, it will be too late.

Those who rear children have a responsibility to society. When their child goes out of control, it affects others in the community, not just them. Children that are out of control generally become teens that are out of control, and these teens will eventually become dysfunctional adults rearing their own children.

Once we begin to value one another and provide accountability and deterrence for every member of society, perhaps there will be a change. A perfect opportunity presented itself a short time ago. I was at the grocery store the day before Thanksgiving, and the crowds were swelling. As I stood in line, a woman's child, approximately four years of age, cried and carried on loudly because she wanted her mother to buy her a video. The woman proceeded to purchase thirteen different gift cards, a process that took an eternity, as the child continued to cry, plead, and beg for the video. It was a tremendous annoyance compounded by the very long line and crowd, but unbelievably, the girl's mother was impervious to the crying. She did not even tell the child to stop.

Finally, I could not handle the crying any more. I spoke up, "Little girl, stop it! We don't want to hear you anymore!" Surprisingly, others in line looked aghast, rather than relieved, that I had chosen to say something. One woman looked at me and said, "You must not have any children." I replied, "I have two, but they don't behave like that." The child appeared briefly effected by what I said. However, since her mother acted as though she did not even hear my comment, she continued her tantrum. After enduring this frustrating event, I watched in horror as the mother walked to the adjacent counter and purchased her daughter the video. This woman had just taught her daughter what to do when she wants something—throw a tantrum until she receives it.

Parents are simply failing to provide needed control for their children, oblivious and unaccountable to others they affect. For example, a short time ago, a child purposely struck my child in the face with a hard toy, with enough force to create an instant bruise. I sat rigid, trying to compose myself, as I tend to react like a violent mama bear when my children are victimized. I was satisfied when my son, through his tears, said, "Why did you do that?" and "You hurt me; say you're sorry!" The child would not apologize, and a grin appeared on his face, which just made my son cry even harder. The mother chided her son and urged him to apologize; when he refused, she told my son, "I'm sorry, he is not ready to apologize." Who is not ready—the child to make amends or the parent to take action and hold her child accountable?

People need to understand the obligation of rearing a child before committing themselves to the task. They will be largely responsible for their child's behavior. Something is going wrong in this area. People do not know how to parent and are producing children with no respect for adult authority or "consequence." Anyone who works with children can attest to the fact that children are becoming more brazen. Recently, I confronted a five-year-old who was mistreating my then three-year-old son. I said, "Johnny, do not pick my son up, throw him on the ground, or even touch him." His reply was, "Why not?" Many schoolteachers report the same flagrant attitude. They complain that when they tell elementary children what to do, they receive responses such as, "I don't have to listen to you," or "You are not my mom."

Children are shooting one another at schools, assaulting teachers, car jacking, and murdering, and what is our response? "He is only fourteen; how can we punish him harshly?" This is the wrong stance to take, as it enables the child to continue unacceptable behavior and go unpunished. Further, it teaches the child that the behavior is tolerable and fails to serve as a deterrent.

The above facts might seem overwhelming. How can there be a solution to such a multifaceted problem? It can start with swift, meaningful consequences that everyone applies, including parents, schools, and courts. Respect, accountability, and deterrence are the cornerstones of meaningful consequences. Respect is gained for the law, entity, or individual upholding the standards of behavior. Accountability emanates from a time of self-reflection, culpability, and remorse. Last, deterrence provides a boundary for behavior and prevents one from repeating mistakes.

Do your part as a parent. Raise your children to respect you, the law, and others. Take an inventory of your parenting style and its effectiveness. If your child is still very young, and you have identified problem areas, involve the child and develop a plan to eradicate the behavior. If your child is a young adult, sit down with him and discuss your thoughts. Ask your child questions you think you already know the answer to, or even questions with answers you do not think you want to know.

Part of my job as a probation officer is to gather information from the incarcerated child and their parent regarding the family dynamic and current delinquency issues. I ask each party the same set of questions, and I am always shocked at the responses I receive. It is as if the family does not even reside in the same household. The parent is oblivious to the child's friends, drug and alcohol use, and other delinquency factors.

I guess the answer to "How to Raise a Juvenile Delinquent" is rather easy. Provide no respect, accountability, or deterrence, provide little supervision to allow your child maximum privacy, enable poor behavior whenever possible, and be inconsistent. Lastly, take no steps to avert problems staring you in the face. Certainly, no one wants to raise a delinquent, but many inadvertently do just that and seem powerless to reverse the problem.

Hopefully, this book will be a small start to solving a problem that is out of control. Let's begin to reverse the effects of time and start picking battles that matter. We should be focusing on providing deterrence and accountability for those who victimize others. We should be focusing on providing education for those venturing into parenthood. We should be holding one another accountable, instead of accepting excuses for unacceptable behavior. We should be ensuring that entities and systems offering accountability are doing it properly. Lastly, we should be focusing on improving our standards of behavior, both individually and collectively.

Remember the concept of R.A.D. and make it an integral part of your child-rearing strategy. Practice proactive parenting and be an active participant in your child's life. Know that without consistency, your efforts to be an effective parent will be hampered. If nothing else, hopefully this book has empowered you and given you back some of your authority as a parent. As the parent, you really do know best, and you really are in charge, despite what some of the "experts" would like you to believe.

It is never too late to become a better parent.

Printed in the United States
97380LV00003B/17/A